RATTLER CREEK

RATTLER CREEK

BEN BRIDGES

A Black Horse Western

ROBERT HALE · LONDON

ISBN 0 7090 5595 1

Robert Hale Limited
Clerkenwell House
Clerkenwell Green
London EC1R 0HT

Photoset in North Wales by
Derek Doyle & Associates, Mold, Clwyd.
Printed and bound in Great Britain by
WBC Book Manufacturers Limited,
Bridgend, Mid-Glamorgan.

For Janet – *always*

ONE

The night I rolled into Wetherby, there was murder in my heart.

I say that, but if I'm honest, I didn't really figure to murder *anyone*, not at first, Oh, once I found the man I was after I was going to rough him up, sure. I was going to teach him a lesson and teach it good. But murder?

No. Murder only crept into it later.

I climbed down off the train, stood for a moment at the far end of the long, warped depot and looked around. We'd just come through an early spring shower and water was still dripping off the carriage roofs and beading the curtained windows, but it hadn't done much to relieve the humidity of the dark Texas night. I glanced up. The last of the clouds were finally scooting away to the south, and stars I knew full-well to be unreachable suddenly looked close enough to pick.

Beside me, the four-carriage train was rolled out like a stretching snake. Oblong blocks of light were slanting from the windows to measure their length across the platform boards and dip their edges into still-quivering puddles, and up at the other end of the platform, the station agent was swinging a bull's eye lantern backwards and forwards to let the engineer know that the train could move out again.

I was the only passenger to alight in Wetherby, which was a middling-sized cow-town down along the Pecos. But that was no surprise. I'd never even heard of the place myself until a fortnight earlier, and yet I'd come better than four hundred miles to reach it, and would have gladly travelled ten times that distance so long as I knew that Clare would be there, waiting for me at trail's end.

The train whistle gave a piercing scream and I saw a spear of steam jet skyward just above the engineer's cab. Then the carriages twitched against each other and the train started to pull out.

I switched my carpetbag from my right hand to my left and watched it resume its wheezing, clanking journey east. In the darkness I couldn't see its wheels. It looked as if it were sliding away on a cushion of steam. The blocks of light raced along the platform beside it, keeping pace with the swaying carriages, alternatively stretching and shrinking as they went spilling into puddles and over swells in the buckled boards.

At last the darkness gobbled them up and, anxious now, I went striding across the groaning planks, feeling self-conscious in my Sunday-best grey suit and string tie because they made me look more like a cattle-buyer than the man I really was, a man who bred and sold cattle for a living, a man of the range.

I went through the station house and out into the cleared yard beyond. The town was waiting for me a couple-hundred yards further down a narrow, brushy roadway. I hauled up again, and took my first look at it.

It was just a wide, rutted street hemmed in on

two sides by shoulder-to-shoulder stores, saloons and gaming houses. False fronts squared up to each other like prizefighters, each giving an impression of size and importance that was just that – false. Sloping shingle roofs glistened wetly in the pale moonlight, while lamplight the same dim yellow colour as mustard twinkled at rain-streaked windows. Mirrored in all the fresh puddles, the dancing flames of the well-spaced street-flares appeared to be standing on their heads.

I caught odd sounds riding the faint breeze – laughter, smashing glass, tinkling pianos, a gently-strummed guitar, the occasional crash of a gunshot, the yapping of stray dogs. Closer to hand I heard the sounds of cattle shifting restlessly in the pens we'd passed on the way in, and the cough-like noises of their bawlings and bellowings.

A loose board behind me gave a sudden protest and I stiffened. An elderly voice said, 'Come far, mister?' I turned my head so that I could focus on the agent. He was tall and thin, and his blue serge uniform swamped him. I nodded and said, 'Far, yeah.'

He opened his mouth to say something more, but before he could engage me in a conversation I wanted no part of, I set off for the town.

But the word echoed inside my head. *Far*. It made me think of distance, and home.

I'd spent much of my life chasing outlaws around the Indian Nations for Hanging Judge Parker, but about four years ago I'd finally quit that line, upped stakes and taken my family southwest. Now I ran my own spread down along the Gila, branding J-Star. It was close to Lordsburg, in the New Mexico Territory, a fine few sections where a man who craved peace and good, honest toil could find both. I'd only been on the move for a couple of weeks, but already I missed it.

But at last I had reached my destination. Any time now, I told myself optimistically, the nightmare would be over, and we could start living our lives normally again, all three of us.

Of course, I had no way of knowing at the time that my troubles were only just beginning.

Like all cowmen, I hated walking. My boots were a rider's boots, with narrow toes and low, underslung heels, and they just weren't made for it. But slowly Wetherby came closer, and I got a better look at it.

I was right. Each side of the street was a cluster of businesses – saloons, eat-houses, billiard halls, a couple of hotels, a theatre. Then came a series of smaller store, now in darkness; a meat market, a druggist's, a millinery, a dry goods. The residential blocks stretched away behind both sides of Main, and a couple of larger houses sat alone on the outermost fringes, their ornate entrances illuminated by gently swinging red lanterns.

I climbed up onto the first boardwalk I came to. It was ten o'clock or a little after, and though most folks were in bed, the central, commercial district was still doing good business. I passed red-faced, fun-seeking men going in groups or singly, a few gamblers, drummers, stumbling drunks, even a couple of obvious sheepmen. Riders jogged past and called greetings to friends or acquaintances. Tethered horses eyed me without much enthusiasm from crowded hitchrails. I paid none of it much mind, for I was too busy searching — searching for a saloon called The Yellow Rose.

A quarter of an hour passed and then I found it.

It looked no different to any other saloon, in any other part of the country. It was perched on the corner of Main and Snyder, broad and tall, with smeared tarpaper windows and rough-hewn, squeaking batwings doors.

I went inside.

The sweet-sour mix of alcohol and cigarette smoke slapped me in the face and made me long for both. Again I told myself that it had been a long journey and that I could use a drink to steady my nerves, but at the same time I was too keyed-up for that, and besides, I didn't want anything dulling my senses. Already I was sweating and my guts were tight, and I kept thinking over and over again, *So ... this is where everything we've been through these last eighteen months comes to an end.*

I shouldered through the press of customers, my eyes searching every face. Five men were sitting at a round, green baize table, drinking, smoking and playing draw poker. A ball was whirring clockwise around a revolving roulette wheel to my right. Billiard balls clicked softly against each other on a high-sided table just inside the doorway, and up on the gas-lit stage at the back of the place, a pianist in sleeve-protectors was accompanying a pro-vocatively-garbed *chanteuse* in a sentimental ballad. I noted idly that she was pretty good, even though nobody else seemed to be paying her much attention.

Then my roving eyes snagged on a girl on the other side of the room and my heart leapt because even though she had her back to me, I knew it was *her*, Clare. She had the same rich auburn hair and the same willowy build that Clare had, and straight away I shoved through the crowd to get to her, ignoring the objections that rose up from the people I pushed inside.

I went up to her, feeling tight in the chest. She was talking with a cowboy. I put my free hand on her arm and started to say her name. 'Clare, honey –'

But when she turned to face me I saw that she wasn't Clare, she didn't look anything like her, and I was more disappointed than I can tell you.

I dipped my head apologetically. 'Uh, sorry ma'am. I thought you was –'

She turned away from me without a word, and she and the cowboy went on talking, just like I wasn't there. I realised then that I was trembling, and told myself I'd better get a grip.

I pushed back the way I'd come and put a boot on the brass rail in front of the bar. The backbar mirror showed me the reflection of a big man with a tanned and weathered face, a set of steel-grey eyes, a straight wedge of nose and a pair of lips that seemed to have taken on the same bronze cast as the rest of the ugly skin around them. He had a handlebar moustache, that ugly-looking bruiser in the mirror, and a little triangular tuft of hair immediately below his bottom lip.

A bartender came over, head tilted back, expression open and expectant as he waited for my order. I reached my free hand up and nudged back my wide-brimmed black Stetson. A lock of loose, sand-coloured hair tumbled down across my forehead. I leaned across the ring-marked mahogany and said, 'I'm looking for Clare Bannon.'

He turned his face so that his ear was pointed directly at me. 'Say what?'

I raised my voice so that he'd hear me above all the other sounds. 'Clare Bannon. She around?'

He turned and stared at me. It was a strange look, and I didn't know what to read into it. He looked at me for a moment more, then licked his lips and said, as tonelessly as he knew how, 'Never heard of her, bub.'

He started to shift away but I stopped him. 'This is The Yellow Rose, isn't it? She told me she worked here.'

Impatiently now, the bartender said, 'Wal, she must of been tellin' you lies, bub. Ain't no Clare Bannon works here.'

'You been here long?'

'Couple months.'

'Maybe I better talk to someone else, then.'

He shrugged. 'It's a free country. But you're wastin' your time.'

Someone yelled for a beer and he hustled away to pull it. I stayed where I was, allowing the crowd to jostle me, and wondered what to make of what he'd told me. I knew Clare wouldn't have lied. She'd been raised right in that regard. Besides which, she'd had nothing to gain by lying. Just the opposite, in fact.

I turned around and put one elbow on the bartop. Even though he'd told me that Clare didn't work there, I had to make sure for myself. The girl on the stage finished her ballad. I think I was the only one who noticed. There was a short pause. I saw disdain on the girl's face as she looked down at her indifferent audience. Then the pianist played a couple of flowery chords and she went straight into another, brighter song.

To the left of the stage, set back in a recess, I spotted a door. I guessed that the feller who owned the place must have his office on the other side of it.

I pushed away from the bar and crossed the sawdust towards it. I got to within a dozen feet of the door and then a brick wall of a man with a prizefighter's face and a suit that couldn't even begin to accommodate all of his muscles stepped into my path.

'Help you, mister?' he asked. He had a low, gravelly kind of voice, and spiky red hair.

'I'd 'preciate a word with the owner.'

He tipped his head back and looked at me in the same speculative way the bartender had. 'What about?'

I opened my mouth, figuring to tell him that was between me and the owner, but then I changed my mind. I didn't need a confrontation. So instead I said, 'I'm looking for Clare Bannon.'

Something came down over his piggy little eyes like a curtain, only it was a thin curtain and I could still see right through it. Warily he said, 'What's your interest in Clare Bannon?'

Something electric washed through me. 'She *is* here, then?'

'Uh-huh. Not any more.'

'She moved on?'

'You *could* say that.'

'She still in town?'

He shook his head. 'You didn't answer my question, friend. What's *your* interest in Clare Bannon?'

Ignoring him, I reached into my pocket and said, 'There's a twenty in it for you if you tell me where I can find her.'

He reached down and clamped one of his big,

lumpy-knuckled hands around my forearm. 'I've ast you twice,' he said in his low, rough-edged voice. 'I don't *never* ask three times.'

I looked up at him, feeling tired and jumpy and short-tempered. It was a long time since I'd felt that way, and feeling like it now made me remember everything that was bad about the life I used to lead.

He released his hold on me and my hand buckled into a fist. I'd come a long way and so far I was no nearer to finding Clare than I had been when I started. Now, I'd just about had enough of it. I was going to hit him. I knew it. I was going to take this lug on and knock some answers out of him, and I didn't give a damn that he was half my age and twice my size, just as long as I got the answers. That's the way I'd always been.

It was about then that I felt a light pressure on my arm, and when I turned my head I saw a pretty young woman standing beside me.

'It's all right, Sam,' she said, addressing the bouncer. 'I'll handle this.'

It took a moment before I realised that she was the girl who'd just been up on the stage, singing. She looked different away from the hiss and flicker of the stage-lights: younger. She looked at me and indicated with a tilt of the head that I should go with her, and I let her lead me away from the big red-head, Sam, and over towards a discreet corner table.

'What'll you have to drink?' she asked, glancing back at me over one bare shoulder.

I said, 'Nothing, I'm here to – '

'I know why you're here,' she cut in. 'Leastways, I *think* I do.' She turned at the waist and lifted a hand, and I saw one of the bartenders nod and then pour a couple of shots of rye.

We reached the table. She told me to sit and I did. She was tall, and her wine-red dress, which had some kind of dyed red plumage around the bust, hugged her hourglass figure like a selfish lover. She was about thirty, I judged. Her skin was bleached by rice powder, and her mouth was a seductive red slash. Her eyes were dark, with long lashes, and her nose was small and neat. She wore her lustrous blonde hair up in a tower of curls and ringlets, and a fake tiara sparkled in the smoky light of the wagon-wheel chandeliers overhead.

The bartender came over and put our drinks down on the table. I flipped a coin onto his tray and he turned and left us. Not once did I take my eyes off the girl.

'You're Allison?' she said after a moment. 'Jim Allison? Clare's father?'

I nodded. 'How – ?'

'She told me you'd be coming for her. She described you.' She held back from saying more, and I saw that same look on her face that I'd seen on the faces of the bartender and the bouncer, the look that said *trouble*.

Reaching a decision, she finally raised her glass and said, 'Better drink up, Mr Allison. I've got some bad news for you.'

Ice-water trickled down my spine. My fingers tightened on the glass in my hand, but I made no move to lift it to my lips.

The girl's bottom lip quivered. Then she said, 'I'm sorry, Mr Allison. Clare ... C-Clare's *dead*.'

*   *   *

There's nothing on earth that can prepare a man for news like that. Uncomprehendingly, I whispered, '*What ...?*'

I got shot once, back in '81. I'd cornered a rapist up on the Kiamichi River and he'd decided to make a fight of it rather than come quietly. To this day I can still hear the wet sound his bullet made thwacking into my side, still feel the white-hot wrench of pain that threw me backwards and tore a scream right out of the pit of my stomach. I thought then that you'd never find a pain quite like it anywhere else.

I was wrong.

Again she said, 'Better drink up.'

This time I did, my actions coming automatic and without conscious effort. The rye burned the back of my throat and settled in my gut like liquid fire, but I didn't feel it. I was still trying to take in what this blonde woman had told me. Clare *dead? Dead?*

No, I thought desperately. *No, you're wrong. You've got to be. Goddlemighty, she's only nineteen!*

The girl bowed her head, and even above all the million-and-one other sounds going on around us, I heard the small sounds she made weeping. Without looking up she said, 'I've been dreading this moment ... having to tell you ... Clare and me, we were good friends, Mr Allison. I felt her pain the s-same way I feel yours.'

Dumbly, my mind slowly recovering from the shock, I said, 'When did it ...?'

She looked up at me, her dark eyes glistening. 'Last Saturday night.'

I put my elbows on the edge of the table and set my head into my hands. Saturday. That was four days ago. I was shaking now, and feeling sick. It was reaction setting in. I wanted to tell her again that she was wrong, that Clare, my little Clare, was still alive. But I knew deep down that she wasn't.

The girl on the other side of the table reached out and put one hand on my left wrist. I was so preoccupied by then that I jumped, and she flinched back from me.

'I'm sorry, Mr Allison,' she said tearfully. 'I'm so sorry.'

My response was another question. 'How did it happen?'

Her face hardened then, and suddenly I saw the real girl beneath all the make-up and finery, the sad, desperate, ill-used girl who sang for men who paid her no mind, and did Lord knew what-all else to earn a living.

'You *know* how it happened,' she replied at last.

I did. I said a name. 'Jay?'

She nodded.

'He ... beat her up. Is that it?' It hurt to ask, but I had to.

She nodded miserably. 'You know what kind of a temper he had on him. When he found out she'd written to you ...'

I sat back, feeling twice my forty-five years. Well, I thought. There it is. Suddenly I was so calm it was frightening. Then I thought about Nan, my wife, and the voice inside my head said, *Aw, jeez ... how am I gonna tell Nan?*

I fixed the girl with another look, and again she recoiled from me, because whatever she read in my expression now scared her bad. I struggled to get everything into perspective. Clare was dead. All right. I couldn't change that. But her husband, Jay

Bannon … he was still alive. And I could damn sure do something to change *that*.

'Where is he?' I asked.

She shook her head and shrugged all in one. 'He left town.'

'I don't suppose you know where he went?'

'Uh-huh.'

I nodded. 'Never mind. I'll find him, sooner or later.'

'I bet you will,' she said.

I got up and grabbed my carpetbag. It was too late to do anything now, except to mourn my daughter, and I wanted very much to be alone to do that. I felt hollow, washed out, suddenly exhausted. But there was something else in me as well, something bad and poisonous that only the death of Jay Bannon could exorcise.

The girl got up with me. I said, 'I 'preciate you telling me. I know it wasn't easy.'

'No easier than being told,' she replied.

I made a helpless gesture. 'I don't even know your name.'

'Connie,' she said. 'Connie Crane.'

I nodded as that sank in. 'Well … I'm obliged to you, Miss Crane. I'd like to stop by and speak to you again before I leave, if that's all right.'

Her eyes searched my face. 'You're going after him right away?'

'Wouldn't you?'

'I guess. But … well, it might not be as simple as that, Mr Allison.'

I frowned. 'What does that mean?'

She glanced around the saloon, at all the high spirits and merrymaking, then said, 'Come with me.'

Lifting her long dress a couple of inches, she set off through the crowd and headed for the batwings. I followed her with a suspicious frown. She pushed through the squeaking doors and I dogged her out onto the boardwalk. The night air had turned cooler at last, and the puddled streets were finally starting to quieten and empty out.

I said, 'Where are we — ?' But her look silenced me.

'Just come with me,' she said.

We turned onto Snyder, which was mostly in darkness now. Gradually the stores thinned out and uneven rows of clapboard houses took their place. She turned left, into a narrow alleyway, and still I followed her, wondering where in hell she was taking me.

The alley stretched for a hundred feet and then fed out onto a backlot. In the moonlight I saw a handful of mean little tumbledown shacks rising out of waving, shin-high grass and brush and assorted mountains of discarded junk.

She led me to the nearest shack. It was in darkness, just like all the others. She opened the door. The leather hinges crackled like dry paper. She fumbled around for the lamp on the table just inside the doorway and I waited outside until I heard the scratch of a match and slowly dull amber light began to illuminate the interior. Then, when she gestured for me to go inside, I did.

The shack smelled musty. I glanced around it, but passed no comment. A few cans sat on a sloping shelf. A greasy range stood unused in one corner. Two ladderback chairs were piled high with balled-up dresses and snake-like feather boas, and little piles of dainty shoes were stacked beneath each of them. An unmade bed dominated the shack, and at the foot of the bed I was surprised to see a wicker bassinet.

Connie took hold of the lamp and held it high, so that the light chased all the shadows out of the crib. Inside it, sleeping peacefully on its belly, I saw a young baby.

I looked at her. 'Yours?' I asked softly.

She shook her head. 'No, Mr Allison. Clare's.'

I stared at her, stunned. '*What?*'

'He's your grandson, Mr Allison,' she said. 'Your grandson James.'

Dumbstruck, I looked at the baby again, closer this time. My *grand*son?

The baby's head was turned to one side and I could see his scrunched-up, pink little face clearly. One of his tiny hands flexed. His fingers took hold of the pillow, then relaxed. A moment later he stirred again, and opened eyes the same light blue as Clare's. He lay staring into space for a moment; then his little fingers stiffened and his face screwed up still further and he opened his mouth and gave a plaintive wail.

Connie Crane said, 'Here,' and passed me the lamp. She scooped the baby up and held him so that his head rested on her shoulder. As she patted him comfortingly on the back, she said, 'I hate to leave him on his own, but there's no-one else to look after him.'

I was staring at the baby, trying to get it into my head that he was my daughter's son, my grandson, the child who had been named James after the grandfather who hadn't even known he existed. I went and put the lamp back on the table, not sure how much more of this I could take.

When the baby's wails died down to a few liquidy gurgles, Connie said, 'Here,' again, and passed him over to me. I took him awkwardly and held him close so that I could feel his tiny heart hammering away against my chest. I looked down into his face. He was about eight or nine months old, I guessed. Now that I knew, I thought I could see a resemblance to Clare in him, but maybe that was just a trick of the light. I held him a little tighter and brushed my palm across his downy brown hair and thought, *Clare ... Aw, Clare ...*

It was then that a sudden, overwhelming rush of emotion washed the baby from my vision, and a sob came up out of my mouth before I could stifle it. I covered as much of my face as I could with my free hand, then turned away from the girl and broke my heart.

A short while later, Connie put one hand on my arm. Her voice was thick with emotion when she said, 'I better get back, Mr Allison.'

I ran my palm down my face, my movements rough and irritable because I hadn't wanted to show myself up like that. Keeping my face turned away from her, I cleared my throat and said, 'All right, Connie. I've got him now.'

'You ... you might as well make yourself at home, try to get some sleep. There's food and coffee, if you need it.'

'What about you?'

'I'll share with one of the other girls for tonight.'

I turned and looked her right in the face this time. 'Thanks.'

She left me alone and closed the door behind her

with a soft click. I took another look around the shack, still rocking the baby in my arms. I'd come to Wetherby prepared for a lot of things, but not this. The baby made a contented little sound and stirred briefly. I looked down at him, listening to the faint suckling sounds he was making, watching as his eyes rolled up and he went back to sleep.

I put him back into the bassinet and covered him over. When I was sure he was sleeping soundly again, I took off my hat and threw it onto one of the chairs. I ran my hands up through my hair, brushing it straight back off my face. I heard it rasp against my cardboard collar, for I wore it long back then.

What was I going to do now? It was a question for which I had no immediate answer.

In the distance I heard the tinkling of a piano and the laughter of men. A church bell tolled the hour. Eleven. I stared up at the shadows shifting around the ceiling and thought some more about Jay Bannon, the father of my grandson, the killer of my daughter.

On impulse I snatched up my carpetbag and threw it onto the bed. I delved inside, shoving my change of clothes aside to get to the bottom. At last my fingers connected with warm leather and cool metal, and I pulled out a gun-filled holster around which was coiled a fully-stocked, forty eight-loop shellbelt.

I hefted the weapon and belt for a couple of seconds, trying to remember the last time I had worn and used it. Then I took out the gun and inspected it. It was a single-action Colt's Army revolver, model of '82, with hard rubber grips into which had been stamped the impression of an eagle with spread wings. I tested the weight and balance of it, ran my eyes along its blued five-inch barrel, then thumbed back the hammer, flipped open the loading gate and turned the cylinder. The gun had been chambered for .476 Eley cartridges, and it had always been my experience that when you hit a man with one of those, he stayed hit.

I set the hammer down on the empty sixth chamber, snapped the loading gate closed and slipped the Colt back into its pouch.

That was the moment when murder really crept into my heart; when I made up my mind that come hell or high water, Jay Bannon was going to die for what he had done – that he was going to die twitching in the dirt with me and my smoking gun looming large above him.

TWO

I coiled the belt back around the gun and put them both back into my carpetbag. Then I took off my jacket, loosened my tie and gently eased myself down onto the unmade bed. All I wanted to do now was sleep and forget. But sleep wouldn't come. Again I wondered how Nan was going to take the news. Just how the hell did you tell a mother that her only child was dead, killed just four days before her father could take her away from the brute she'd married?

My sigh filled the room.

Without meaning to, I found myself thinking about Jay Bannon. I pictured him in my mind. What was it that women saw in men like that?

He'd come into our lives on a warm mid-summer's evening in 1887. It had been the usual active, dawn-to-dusk kind of day, and we were just sitting down to supper, Nan, Clare and me, when we heard the sounds of a horse being walked into the yard.

Visitors had never been plentiful in those parts, so I got up, threw down my napkin and went outside – and there he was, sitting his mount right out front, slouched in his saddle, arms crossed over the pommel, looking exhausted and trying hard to fight it.

Behind him, the sky was a series of ragged streamers – gold, amber, red and powder blue, with patches of orange-white cloud hanging motionless high over the rich canyon country.

I looked at his horse first, because you can tell a lot about a man from his horse. It was a shaggy-haired, ungainly pony with a dark, unkempt mane and a tail that practically swept the ground when it walked. In better times it had likely been a durable mount, but now it looked underfed and frankly worthless.

Next I checked his clothes; a flat-crowned, narrow-brimmed black hat, a dark velvet jacket that had seen much use, an old blue bib-style shirt and threadbare woollen trousers. He wasn't armed, so far as I could see.

Finally I looked at the man himself.

He was twenty four or five. When Nan and Clare came out onto the porch to see who had come calling, he doffed his hat and offered them a polite smile. He had a mop of curly blue-black hair, two very bright, penetrating brown eyes, a long, straight nose and a wide mouth. It had been at least a day since he'd shaved, and there was a dull shadow sketching his jaw.

He introduced himself as Jay Bannon from California, and asked if there was any work to be had. There wasn't. I ran a little over a thousand head of cattle and employed two men to help me with them. Round-up, branding, the drive to market, they were all behind us now, and there weren't enough chores left over to justify hiring another hand.

I told him as much and he took it with a slow

nod, but he was obviously disappointed, and there was no doubt that he was down on his luck.

'Thanks anyway, mister,' he said, gathering his reins back up. 'I ... I'm sorry to've troubled you. Ladies.'

He made to turn his horse away but on impulse Nan, a small, sturdy, proud-looking woman with red hair and blue eyes, stopped him. She'd noticed the lean, gaunt look of him, and though she could be tough as nails when she had to be, there was a soft and charitable side to her as well.

'Mr Bannon,' she said in her customary soft, cultured Irish brogue. 'May I ask you something?'

He looked down at her and said cautiously, 'I guess.'

'When was the last time you ate?'

He smiled bitterly. 'Aw, don't you worry – '

'When?'

He paused. Then; 'Day before yesterday.'

'Then you must be just about ready for some good homecooked food, I'm thinking.'

'Aw no, I couldn't – '

But Nan would hear no protest. Her mind was made up. 'Clare – set an extra place for Mr Bannon.'

And that was how he came into our lives. He dismounted and made to follow the women inside, but I stopped him with a quiet word, and when he turned to me I told him he should put his horse up in the barn first, alongside the ranch-stock, and fill a spare bin with grain.

He looked at me queerly, then. It was obvious that he hadn't even considered the care of his mount.

At last he nodded and did as I'd suggested, then

he came inside and we all sat down to steak and potatoes, and in between mouthfuls he told us something about himself, about how he was good with ciphers and had been trying to hunt up gainful employment as a book-keeper right across the southwest, without much success.

I didn't eat much that evening, I just sat there nursing coffee and letting my eyes roam around the table while he talked. It wasn't hard to see that Nan and Clare had taken an instant shine to him. He had that way with him. He could be real plausible when he wanted to be, and he knew his manners. Out west, women who knew only rough and ready men like me set a lot of store by that.

He wolfed down his food and passed all kinds of compliments about it, and though Nan told him he was being too kind, I could see that she appreciated the flattery. As for Clare, well ... she hung on his every word, because he was a good talker and he'd seen quite a bit of life on his travels, whereas she had learned very little because of the lonely, sheltered life she'd always known with us.

With the meal finally out of the way, we retired to the porch to smoke and watch the sun drop down behind the far, jagged peaks and flat-topped mesas. He took a long, thin cigar from his shirt pocket and bit the end off with strong, even teeth. He said he'd been saving it for a special occasion, and now was as good a time as any to fire it up. Silently I stuffed my pipe with rough-cut tobacco and soon we were both filling the sunset with our smoke.

It was a cool, peaceful evening. Lowing cattle set up a distant accompaniment to the nearer zip of scavenging flies and the stamp and shift of the horses in the barn and corral. Down at the far end of the bunkhouse, woodsmoke puffed out of the rock chimney and I smelled burning bacon on the sweet evening air. That would be Jorge Canedo, I thought with a wry shake of the head. Jorge never could cook worth a damn. My other man, Tom Jessup, was already out riding nighthawk on the herd, and I could hear him blowing a sad cowboy melody on his harmonica.

After a time I indicated the bunkhouse with the stem of my pipe and said, 'When you're ready, go across and introduce yourself to Jorge. Tell him I said you could make yourself at home for the night.'

I felt Jay looking at my profile. He was as tall as me, but with a much slimmer build. 'Thanks, Mr Allison,' he said after a while. 'You people ... you been real kind to me.'

I gave him a rough shrug. Tell you the truth, I was annoyed with myself for being so damned soft, because even then I knew there was something about him I couldn't trust. I guess I'd spent so many years as a lawman that after a while it got so you could tell almost at a glance.

But then I reminded myself that I hadn't packed a badge for almost three years, and I'd mellowed out a bit. And, like I've already said, Bannon was a young man down on his luck. He was at that stage of his life when he could've gone either way, and there was no telling what difference a little kindness might make.

'I'll pay you back, soon as I can,' he said.

I looked at him then. 'I don't want payment, son.'

'Maybe not. But there must be something needs doing around here. I'll be honest with you, Mr

Allison. I'm no great shakes on the back of a horse. But I can use my hands. You show me something needs fixing, I'll fix it.'

In spite of my misgivings, I smiled. 'We'll see. Goodnight, Jay.'

Next morning I rose early, washed, pulled my shirt on over my head and fired up the range for coffee. While I was waiting for the water to boil, I caught the sounds of someone skulking around in the backyard, and stiffened. Before I got to the door there came a sudden *whack-thud, whack-thud*. Frowning now, I eased open the door and peered outside.

There, in the clean, pale light of dawn, I saw Bannon stripped to the waist, setting up and splitting logs for firewood. I watched him for a while, thumb-scratching the little tuft of sand-coloured hair just below my bottom lip. He didn't know I was there, because he had his back to me.

Then I turned and went back into the house, thinking that maybe I'd misjudged him after all.

I don't know just how Jay Bannon became a more or less permanent fixture around the place. He just *did*. He turned his hand to anything I told him to do and he did the best job he had in him. It wasn't always up to the mark, true, but at least he tried, and in my book that counted for a lot.

Nan and Clare thought the world of him. I guess that after me and the hired men, he was like a breath of fresh air. He was intelligent and worldly, and he could regale the women with all kinds of tall stories. He knew a lot about foreign lands and he would throw odd little facts into whatever conversation you might be having and automatically take it over. Say for instance you happened to mention New Year. Straightaway Jay would pipe up with, 'You know, in Hungary they let a pig run through the house on New Year's Eve and then try to touch its tail so they'll have good luck.'

Yep – he was good company and he always tried his best. But there was still something about him that I just couldn't take to.

One evening about a week and a half later, Tom Jessup came over to see me. Tom was a tall, whip-lean, bow-legged man with a big, lumpy face, a wide, black-turning-to-grey moustache and a once-broken nose. He was a couple of years younger than me, with a deep, slow Texas drawl and a kindly nature. We'd both ridden for Judge Parker back in the old days, and because he also knew cattle, we'd asked him to come with us when we finally decided to move south and west and get into the ranching business. Tom'd had enough of being shot at in the Nations, same as me, and he'd said yes.

I was sitting out on the porch, one leg braced against the rail, smoking my after-supper pipe, and I nodded a greeting when he was close enough. ''Tom. Set a spell.'

He shook his head beneath his big suede and tasselled Plainsman, and folded his arms across the porch-rail instead. 'Naw, I ain't stoppin'.'

At the back of the house, Nan and Clare laughed at something Jay said to them. The laughter had a pleasant sound as it rode the warm evening breeze, but when he heard it, I saw Tom wince.

'Something on your mind?' I asked.

He looked uncomfortable, and shook his head. 'Naw, I's just wonderin', was all.'

'Wondering what?'

'How long you're fixin' to let that new feller stay around here.'

I sat forward and took the pipe from my mouth. 'Jay? What makes you ask a question like that?'

He was clearly reluctant to come right out with it, whatever *it* was. 'Aw, nothin'. Just wondered is all.'

'Come on, Tom. Spit it out.'

'Well … I wouldn't want to get him into any trouble. An' I'll be straight with you, Jim – I'm not even sure it *was* him, but …' He made the sort of helpless, embarrassed gesture that inarticulate men make all the time.

'What are you trying to say, Tom?'

He glanced around to make sure he wouldn't be overheard, then leaned forward over the porch-rail and said, 'You call a man a thief, that's a mighty serious charge. So don't get me wrong. I ain't comin' right out an' sayin' that. But … well, they's some money gone missin' from my poke.'

I narrowed my eyes at him. Tom had elderly parents living down in Presidio who were no longer able to support themselves. He held back part of his wages every month, kept it stuffed into an old sock under his mattress, and when he had enough he wired it down to them. He never made any secret of it. There was never any need. Until now …

'I's jus' checkin' up to see how much I had,' he went on. 'I got a rough idea, but I jus' thought I'd make sure.' He turned his mild blue-grey eyes up to me. 'It's light about twenty dollars,' he went on. 'An' that's not all. I got the damnedest feelin' someone's been through my gear, you know, riflin' in. An' Jorge says his stuff's been disturbed, too.'

I let that sink in. Any way you cut it, Jay Bannon was the likeliest suspect, although I hated to jump to that sort of conclusion. Still, who else could it have been? Nan? Clare? *Me?* No; over the last three years, we'd grown close, the lot of us. We were more like family.

'You want me to have a word with him about it?' I asked at length.

'Naw. I got no real proof, an' I'd hate like hell to make trouble. But I don't mind tellin' you, Jim, I'll feel a sight happier when he's gone.'

I nodded. Under any other circumstances, I knew that Tom would have taken care of this business in his own quiet way, without bringing me into it at all. But because Bannon had quickly ingratiated himself with the women and he had no wish to upset them, he'd chosen to do nothing more than tell me discreetly what had happened. I appreciated that.

'I'll make it up to you, Tom,' I said. 'What was it, twenty dollars?'

'I don't want your money, Jim.'

'I know. But you'll get it, anyway.'

My pipe had gone cold. I reached forward and knocked the dottle out of it, then blew through the stem a couple of times, knocked it out into my palm twice and then slipped it into my shirt pocket. 'Keep an eye on him, Tom,' I said. 'I will, too. First sign it looks like he's stealing, he's out of here.'

But there weren't any more incidents like that, leastways none than ever came to light, and things more or less carried on the way they had been for the next several days.

No matter what Tom or Jorge or I might have thought about Bannon, however, he was honest about one thing — I've never seen a man so completely down-to-the-ground useless aboard a horse. I tried to make a cowboy out of him, but it was a vain effort. I guess that's why he'd been trying to chouse up work as a book-keeper.

Then, around the middle of the third week, I found out something else about him, too.

Something altogether darker.

Some of my stock had been spotted straying onto the main Glenwood-Lordsburg trail, and when I rode out to investigate, I found that a part of my boundary fence had come down. Since I had no desire to let my stock become a nuisance or a danger to all the mail coaches, bullwhackers and muleskinners who used the trail, I figured I'd better repair it p.d.q.

I told Jay it looked like we'd be spending the rest of the week digging and stringing.

It was a good late-August morning when we loaded up the wagon with all our tools and materials and set off. There was a lazy warmth to the day that was typical of New Mexico at that time of year. The cloudless sky was azure blue, the distant mountains of powdery purple, the nearer, weather-seamed mesas a mixture of orange and brown. In the distance, away on the other side of a rolling stretch of mesquite grass, scattered pockets of cottonwood, pinon and juniper provided the only shade for miles around.

For once, Jay was holding his peace. I remember thinking that it made a pleasant change, because by then he'd worn out his smooth-talking welcome with everyone but Clare. I'd started to get the feeling that he'd had his fill of ranch-work, too — that hard, physical work of *any* description would never set well with him, except when he was trying to impress. Given the choice, he would sooner be at the house, just loafing around and shooting the breeze with Clare, or trying to worm his way back into Nan's affections with his oily, easy compliments.

Well, that was too bad. After that business with Tom Jessup's savings, I'd put him on wages. I don't know why. I guess I still had it in my mind that he was young and insecure and that he could still go either way. But as long as he was taking my money, he could take my orders as well. If he didn't like it, all he had to do was quit.

It was a little after eight when we reached the gentle ridge where a goodly portion of the fence had come down. We hopped down from the wagon and studied the job for a while, then set to, digging out and clearing away all the rotten posts in readiness for sinking in some replacements.

The morning wore on and grew warmer. We would have worked in silence but for the fact that Jay grumbled about everything I asked him to do. Sometime around midday we broke for something to eat and drink, and hunkered for a time in the shade of the wagon, to cool off. In the distance cattle bellowed. We spotted a bottle-green stage-coach and a high-sided freight wagon rumbling along the trail half a mile or so beyond us. Jay still had very little to say for himself, and neither was I in much of a mood of conversation.

Then, right out of the blue, Jay looked across at me and said, 'I don't know about you, Mr Allison, but I've had my fill of this job. You mind if I head on back, now?'

I regarded him over the lip of my canteen. For a moment there I thought he was kidding with me, but when I looked him in the face I saw that he really meant it, and I was stunned. Out here, men and women just bit the bullet, pulled together and got the job – whatever it was – done. You didn't just get so far, then decide you'd had enough and leave the other poor bastard to it, especially when you were only the hired man. It just wasn't the way.

I stoppered the canteen and slowly put it down. Then I said mildly but firmly, 'Matter of fact, Jay, I *do* mind.' I nodded towards the work we'd done so far. It wasn't much. 'We haven't even *started* yet.'

He followed my line of vision, his face tight, flushed and sweaty. 'It sure is a bitch of a job, though,' he muttered sourly.

'It is, that. But it's got to be done.'

I climbed back to my feet and slapped the dust off the seat of my pants. He lingered where he was for a while longer, then finally dragged himself erect and followed me back to work.

The afternoon stretched on. The old posts were stubborn and didn't want to come up. Jay continued to bitch under his breath. I don't know that he was being deliberately uncooperative, but for sure he only did what I told him to do, and no more.

At last we threw all the old lumber into a pile and dug some new holes. By late afternoon, with the sun slanting our elongated shadows away to the east, we were ready to start hammering in the new posts.

Jay's attitude had irritated the hell out of me, but I tried not to let it show. As we unloaded the new posts from the back of the wagon, I offered him a choice — he could hold the posts in place while I hammered them down, or vice versa.

'You hold,' he grunted back. '*I'll* hammer.'

In all we knocked in three posts, me wrapping my gloved hands midway around each in turn and holding them straight while Jay swung my big twenty-five-pound sledgehammer. For a man who didn't like work, Jat had taken the hardest job of the lot, swinging that hammer up and bringing it down on top of the post, then doing it all over again until we had a foot or eighteen inches under the ground. It was a tough chore, and I knew from experience that every time you hit the post you felt the impact travel right up your arms and across your back.

The hammer came down again and again with a peculiarly hollow *POCK-AH* sound that swept out over the range and then bounced back as from a vast distance, *pock-ah* … I crouched beside Jay, sweating as he was sweating, feeling every impact shivering up my arms and across my shoulders just as he was, *POCK-AH* … *pock-ah* … *POCK-AH* … *pock-ah* … I listened to the push and draw of his breath as he swung and hammered, swung and hammered. Slowly, quarter-inch by quarter-inch, the post sunk deeper into the ground.

And then I frowned.

Suddenly I realised that Jay was whispering in time to his actions, '… come on, you bastard … come on, you bastard … come on, you bastard … '

POCK-AH … *pock-ah* … *POCK-AH* … *pock-ah* …

Carefully I glanced up at him. I don't think I've ever seen so much fury in another man's face in all my life. His dark, penetrating eyes fairly burned into the post, and beneath his snarling lips his teeth were clenched. It was as if he were directing all of his hatred at that one column of wood.

The hammer kept rising, swinging and falling, *POCK-AH ... pock-ah ...* and Jay kept hissing, '... come on, you bastard ... come on, you bastard ... come on, you bastard ...'

I had never seen behaviour like it before. Even as I watched, I could see the anger and hatred taking firmer hold of him. Sweat was flying off his brow, his eyes were glazing, almost seeming to stand out from their sockets, his jaw muscles were twitching and dancing ...

'*... come on ...*'

... POCK-AH ... pock-ah ...

At last I let go of the post and stood up. 'All right, Jay,' I said, a little scared of him, and for him. 'That's enough now.'

He didn't hear me. He brought the sledgehammer down again, again, again, his stare intense and unblinking, his lips twitching and jerking, his teeth biting down hard, his voice growing louder, harsher –

I took a step away from him, for he was in a really murderous rage now, and again I said, 'All right, Jay, that's *enough!*'

He brought the hammer down one last time, in such a temper now that he completely missed the pulped top of the post and accidentally struck the ground at his feet instead. Frowning, I started to ask him what the hell had gotten into him, but he wasn't through yet. Suddenly he raised the hammer again and roared something I couldn't quite make out, then swung it sideways on at the post and slammed it slantwise.

I said, 'What in the *hell* – ?'

But he roared again and hit the post again and it bent even further over to one side, and splintered along one edge.

'*Bastard* …!' he screamed, spit flecking his lips now. '*Bastard* … *bastard* … *BASTARD* …!'

I'd never seen anything like it. He was uncontrollable, gripped by some kind of destructive fever, and as I watched him, I got the craziest notion that it was *me* he was calling a bastard, that it was *me* he thought he was hitting, not the post.

He hit the post twice more. It snapped and crashed sideways, part of the edge now completely pulped and flattened. At last, seeing my chance, I threw myself forward and grabbed him in such a way as to pin his arms to his sides. We tumbled over in a heap, our hats going flying, and he let go of the hammer. We wrestled for a wild few moments, until I had him flattened out on the ground.

I glared down at him, getting angry myself now. His face was contorted and hideous, home to all that was vicious and evil. I yelled, 'For crissakes, Jay, what's the *matter* with you?'

He shoved me sideways and, taken by surprise, I fell away from him. The next thing I knew, he was back on his feet and kicking me in the stomach, screaming, '*Bastard* … *bastard* … *bastard* …!'

Confused and hurting, I tried to back away from him but still he came after me, so I had no choice but to defend myself. I caught hold of his boot, twisted it hard and thrust him backwards, and while he was off-balance, I climbed back onto my feet and went after him.

His face was suffused with blood, so that in the crimson cast of the sinking sun he looked like a demon from hell. He came at me with his fists flailing, but I blocked his first roundhouse right and whacked him right on the jaw. He spun around and his legs went out from under him. When he rolled onto his back there was blood all over his mouth and his chest was heaving. He was still mad, but I could see that I'd finally knocked some of the pepper out of him.

I stood above him, big hands clenched, ready to dish out some more if he wanted it. Again I said, 'What the hell's got into you, Jay?'

He spat off to one side and wiped his mouth with the back of one hand, smearing the blood across his cheek. If looks could kill, I'd've been ripe for burying. But other than that, he made no attempt to reply, to explain, to apologise.

Reaching a decision I said, 'Get up.'

He looked at me from under lowered brows.

I said, 'Get up, Jay. Now, I don't know what's eating at you, and to be honest, I don't really care. But I need men I can trust and rely on, and you're not one of 'em. So I'm taking you back to the ranch and paying you off. I want you to collect your gear and then get the hell off my land!'

Still gasping, he got up and stood before me, his expression defiant. 'Paying me off, are you?' he husked. 'Well, could be Clare might have something to say about that.'

I stiffened at the mention of her name, because I'd always been over-protective of her, I guess. 'What's that supposed to mean?'

He smirked at me. 'You mean you don't *know?*' He pawed at his face some more. 'Hell, Allison, you might still think of Clare as your little gal, but take it from me … she's a woman now.'

I knew what he meant to imply by that, of course, but I didn't believe it. I didn't *want* to believe it. 'You better button your lip,' I said in a low voice, 'while you still got a lip to button.'

He shrugged. 'Why don't you ask her?' he invited, enjoying himself now. 'Ask her what me and her got up to all them times you thought she was just showing me around your land. Ask her what we did in your barn, or right out here in the middle of all this open country, or in her own *bed*, with you and your wife fast asleep in the room next door!'

I blurred forward and hit him in the face. He squawked and went down beneath a storm of punches. I couldn't believe it. No father wants to believe something like that, not when his little girl had always been so sweet and pure and –

I guess I lost my head for a while, only seconds, but it seemed more like eternity. When I stepped away from him he was rolling around and cursing me. My fists were throbbing and I was pulling down air like a drowning man.

'You're lying,' I snarled. I didn't really expect an answer. I was just trying to convince myself.

I grabbed him by his shirt and threw him up into the back of the wagon. He flopped around and made a lot of weak, watery groaning noises. I spat into the grass but I couldn't get rid of the sour taste on my tongue. All I wanted was to get shut of him. I gathered all the gear together and threw it into the wagon beside him or on top of him. Then I climbed up onto the seat and turned us around and pointed us back towards the ranch.

I was trembling.

* * *

'No, Daddy! You can't just make him leave!'

It was later. I was standing out front of the house and Jay was just a slow-moving dot on the horizon, a dot that was growing smaller all the time.

We'd arrived back at the ranch about twenty minutes earlier and I'd sent him packing, just like I'd said I would. On the way in he'd moaned and groaned in back of the wagon for a while. Then, when he realised that wasn't going to get him anywhere, he'd tried to turn on the charm again. Crawling across the bed of the wagon, he'd struggled to his feet and clambered over the seat to sit beside me. Feeling his jaw, he'd croaked, 'Mr Allison, you … got to believe me. I just don't know what got into me. Maybe it was the heat. I'm not used to working out of doors, remember …'

I glanced at him. His face was bruised and battered, and blood was crusting over on one of his torn lips. 'Save your breath, Jay. I've made up my mind. I want you off my land by sundown.'

At once his character changed again. He spat off to the side and hissed, '*Damn* you, then!'

Now I watched the immensity of the wide open spaces swallow him up. The last time I saw him, he was hunched in his saddle, filled with spite, jabbing his horse in the flanks to keep it moving at a walk away from the ranch, its long dark tail sweeping the ground as it went.

'*Daddy!*'

I tensed. Clare's voice was hoarse and her tone was verging on the hysterical. I stayed where I was for a moment. I didn't want to look at her right away, not after what Jay had said. But then I turned around. She and her mother were standing on the porch, Clare gripping onto an upright for support, Nan standing beside her, her expression grim, worried, angry.

I looked at my daughter. Clare was tall and slender, with rich auburn hair pinned up above a pale, oval face. Even now I can see the rash of freckles that splashed up and over her snubbed nose, the broad smile that always tugged at her well-proportioned, heart-shaped lips, the firm, determined chin she'd inherited from her mother. She was wearing a simple pink calico dress, but as I looked at her it was as if I was seeing the woman she had become for the very first time, and I felt as if I'd lost something – which, of course, I had.

'Daddy,' she begged. 'Y-you *can't* just s-send him away!'

'*Watch* me,' I replied in a choked kind of whisper.

Relenting a little, I went up onto the porch and reached out to put a hand on her shoulder. She flinched away from me and Nan said, '*Clare!*'

Clare turned and went into the house. We followed her inside. Darkness was stealing rapidly across the countryside by then, and Nan went straight over to the peg lamps fixed over the fireplace and struck a match.

Tearfully Clare said, 'You … can't send him away, Daddy! I … I I-love him!'

I snorted. My knuckles were still stinging from the beating I'd given him, and I sucked on them for a couple of seconds. 'You might *think* you love him,' I replied, 'but you wouldn't've found him so lovable this afternoon. Judas Priest, the sonofabuck was more like a lunatic!'

Light blossomed in the room and shone on the

tears coursing down Clare's face. She was just on seventeen, neither girl nor woman but something painful in between. Realising that, some of the choler seeped out of me and my bunched muscles relaxed. I reached up and thumb-scratched the hair beneath my lower lip, and then said quietly, 'Now listen here, Clare. According to Jay, you and him've been getting up to all sorts around here these past couple weeks. Maybe he was lying, or exaggerating. Maybe he wasn't. I don't want to know. All I want is for you to promise me something.'

She looked at me across the room, her face still so young and naive, the girl herself still so easily led.

'Don't think you've got to give yourself to the first man who comes along,' I said. 'Have more respect for yourself. And show some for us, as well.'

Tears spilled from her light blue eyes.

'Promise me?' I said determinedly.

But she only turned and fled to her room, trying vainly to trap a sob in her throat.

She went missing two days later. At first I thought she'd just taken it into her head to run away. She'd been subdued and moody ever since Jay had gone, but we'd expected that, just like we'd expected that sooner or later she would snap out of it and return to something more like her old self. I figured I would ride out and round her up and bring her home and give her the talking-to she had coming.

But then Jorge Canedo drew my attention to some tracks at the side of the house, just outside her bedroom window, and some more inside the barn, and something wet and slimy unfolded inside me.

Jay had come back. For her. Jay had taken my little girl away from us. And she had gone willingly, believing herself to be misunderstood and in love.

Even now my fists clench just at the thought of it. Because I knew that Jay hadn't come back for her out of love.

No, not him.

He'd come back and taken her away from us out of *spite*.

THREE

I guess you pretty well know the rest of it.

By my reckoning, Jay and Clare had at least an eight or ten-hour start on us, but we figured we could make that up easily enough because we were born horsemen, Tom, Jorge and me, and we knew the country well. We saddled up and followed their tracks west, but somewhere along the line they gave us the slip. After that we split up and over the next couple of days checked out all the settlements and towns within a fifty or sixty-mile radius.

There was no trace of them.

Still, I wasn't through yet. I'd built up quite a few contracts in the law-enforcement business, and in the weeks that followed, Nan and me sent letters to as many of them as we could, explaining what had happened and asking them to keep an eye open for anyone fitting Clare's description.

We didn't hear anything for a couple of weeks. Then I received a letter from a marshal up in Dove Creek, Colorado. He hadn't seen Clare or Jay, but he said he'd certainly heard of Jay. Although there was no paper out on him, he'd assaulted a local wheelwright about six months before, and pretty near beat him to death over some imagined slight. There had also been a number of petty thefts in the town at around the same time, and upon making further enquiries, the marshal had discovered that Jay had quite a history of violent and larcenous behaviour. According to some of the people in his home town of Bisley, California, he was a mite touched in the head.

All of that came as quite a shock, as you can imagine. Looking back on it now, I don't know how we kept from going crazy ourselves. But I never lost hope that Clare would eventually see for herself what kind of a man she'd imagined herself to be in love with, and decide to come back home. Likewise, I always made it a point to ask after her or Jay in every town my business took me to, albeit always in vain.

The better part of a year and a half went by. Then, just a couple of weeks earlier we'd had a note from Clare. She and Jay had gotten married and were now living in a town called Wetherby, down in Texas. Jay worked as a fåro dealer in a saloon called The Yellow Rose, and he'd put her to work there as well. She never said what she did, and part of me didn't want to know. She never said a word about a baby, either. I guess she figured we could only take one shock at a time.

The tone of the letter quickly turned grim. She confessed that Jay beat her regularly, and after much soul-searching she'd decided to leave him. She said she'd been a fool, that she never should have gone away with him in the first place, and that if we could find it in our hearts to forgive her, would I please come and fetch her home.

If we could *forgive* her …

Hell, I set out for Wetherby that very same day.

But like I said, you know the rest of it, what was

waiting for me at trail's end. The only question left
now was, what did I intend to *do* about it?

I must have fallen into a light sleep sometime
around two or three in the morning, because the
next time I opened my eyes, watered-down
dawn-light was falling in through the narrow,
curtainless window and Connie Crane was looking
down at me with concern plain on her personable
face.

For a moment I wasn't sure where I was, or who
she was. Then it all came back to me in a rush and I
made a painful groaning sound behind my teeth
and swung my feet over the edge of the mattress.

'You all right, Mr Allison?' she asked, stepping
back.

'Jim,' I corrected her. 'Yeah, I'm fine.'

She was still wearing the same wine red dress
she'd been wearing the evening before. In the pale
light it looked creased, and her thick blonde hair
was in disarray where she must have slept rough.
She went to the foot of the bed and took the baby
out of the bassinet. 'He didn't give you any
trouble?'

'He was good as gold.'

'Can I fix you some breakfast?'

I shook my head. 'I'm not hungry.'

'Well,' she replied, 'I know a little feller here who
is.'

Cradling the baby on her hip, she went over to
the range and made herself busy with some milk in
a pan. I watched her for a few moments. I felt
lousy. I needed to wash and shave and get out of
my suit and into something more comfortable. I

said, 'Is there anywhere around here that I can change my clothes?'

'Just go right ahead,' she replied without turning around. Then, trying to lighten the atmosphere in the mean little shack, she added, 'I promise not to peek.'

I stood up, grabbed my carpetbag and took out my spare duds. I took off my Sunday-best gear and threw it onto the bed, then hurriedly hauled on and bucked up my black canvas pants. My boots came next, and then, bare-chested, I carried my shaving tackle across to the sawbuck table beside the range and poured cold water from a chipped jug into a chipped bowl.

Once I was through, I rinsed off the remains of the shaving soap, dried my face on a towel that Connie kept on a nail nearby and went back to the bed to finish dressing. I buttoned up a collarless striped cotton shirt, tied my neckerchief and finally strapped on my gunbelt.

I was just settling the holster comfortably against my left hipbone, where I wore it at an angle for a cross-draw, when Connie glanced over one shoulder and asked if she could fix me some coffee.

I looked back at her. She was staring at the Colt, at the big, lean rangeman into which the clothes had transformed me. I said, 'Coffee sounds good, yeah.'

She handed the baby across to me, then gave me his bottle. I went and sat at the corner end of the table and watched him suck hungrily at the teat. He was more precious than I can tell you, because he was the only thing we had left to remind us of Clare. But he was also a burden I could do without if I were to go after Bannon and stand any chance at all of catching up with him.

Connie came over with two steaming cups, then sat opposite me. I stirred sweetening into my cup, feeling her brown eyes watching me. At last, to get the conversation started, she said, 'So.'

I looked over at her. 'So what?'

Under her pretend lightness she looked bleak. 'Have you made up your mind what you're going to do?'

'I *told* you what I'm going to do.'

'That was before you knew you had a grandchild.'

I tried the coffee, then said quietly, 'I know.' I drank some more. On my lap, James made some gurgling, contented sounds. 'Would you look after him for me?' I asked. 'While I'm gone?'

She shook her head.

'Why not?'

'Because you might not come back, and then where would I be?' She sipped her own coffee. 'I can't afford to be saddled with a baby, Mr Allison.'

'Jim,' I corrected again. 'Well, will you at least look after him for today?'

'You know I will. Where will you be?'

I shrugged. 'I just want to have a look around.'

She nodded, guessing what I meant. 'The cemetery's about half a mile south,' she replied. 'Give me a chance to put on something more respectable and I'll take you there, if you like.'

I nodded glumly. 'Thanks.'

Clare's grave was a narrow little mound of earth crowned by a flimsy-looking wooden cross into which had been burned her name and the years of her birth and death. A few drooping flowers projected from the neck of a little blue china vase at the foot of the plot. When I raised an eyebrow to Connie, she nodded and said simply, 'She always liked flowers. At the end I was the only one around to make sure she had some.'

I nodded. 'You were a good friend to her, Connie. You've been a good friend to me as well.'

I returned my eyes to the cross. It was hard to believe that my little girl lay under this oblong of muddy, still-settling dirt. I turned my hat in my hands, trying to communicate with her, trying to tell her that she never should have worried because we'd forgiven her a long time ago, that me and her mother would always love her, that we would take care of the baby, so she needn't concern herself on that score, either.

At length James started to grow restless in Connie's arms, and I put my hat back on and took him away from her. 'Come on,' I said. 'Let's get you two back home.'

We retraced our steps back to town. The morning was warming up and left-over puddles were already starting to steam. The town was busy, and in my arms my grandson watched it all curiously through eyes as round as saucers.

We got about three-quarters of the way back to the shack when I spotted the town marshal's office on the other side of the street. On impulse I slowed to a halt and Connie, looking altogether more demure by now in a light green Dolly Varden dress and a jockey hat, looked a question at me. I nodded to the single-story brick building now directly opposite. 'Think I'll have a word with the local law while I'm here,' I said. 'What's his name?'

'Torrance,' she replied. 'Burt Torrance.'

I passed James over to her. His little fingers went stiff and a look of alarm passed across to his face, because he wasn't completely sure what was happening to him.

'See you later,' I said.

We split up. I crossed the wide dirt road, stepped up onto the far boardwalk and let myself into the office.

Torrance was sitting behind a big, blocky desk just left of a closed door that probably led through to a cellblock and backyard. He appeared to be a tall, underfed, hatless man of forty summers, with a pale, slack face and heavily-oiled brown hair. He was lounging in his shirtsleeves, and when I came inside he looked up from the Montgomery Ward catalogue he'd been studying and threw me a searching squint.

"Morning, stranger. Help you?'

I said, 'Like to ask you a few questions about the murder you had here a few nights ago, marshal.'

He frowned. 'Murder? What murder?'

'Clare Bannon.'

He eyed me blankly. 'Who's Clare Bannon?'

The fact that her name genuinely seemed to mean nothing to him angered me. 'Her husband beat her to death last Saturday night, then lit out for parts unknown,' I replied tightly. 'Sound familiar now?'

He eyed me with renewed interest, but passed no comment on my sarcasm. 'Oh,' he said after a while. '*Bannon*.' He closed the catalogue, stood up and came around the desk with his thumbs hooked in the arm-holes of his grey vest. 'What about it?' he asked.

'I'd like to know what kind of an investigation you carried out.'

'Investigation?'

'You *did* investigate it?'

Now he bristled. 'I investigated,' he said frostily. 'But maybe you don't understand how things are here in Wetherby, mister ...?'

I didn't give him the name he was angling for, I just said, 'Maybe you better tell me, then.'

He did. He said, 'This is a cattle town, case you haven't noticed. We got seventeen saloons of one size or another, and twice that many gambling houses, billiard halls and brothels. Now, we get five or six herds through here all at oncet, that's near-on two hundred extra men need accommodating, and just like all the local cowboys, miners, soldiers and sheepmen, they're each of 'em looking for two things – liquor and fun. Hell, someone gets hurt every hour of the day when it's like that. I look into as much of it as I can, but I'm only one man, and when you're talking about something like the Bannon business ...'

Something moved in my eyes, something dangerous. 'Yeah?'

Torrance shrugged. 'Well, we try not to waste too much time on episodes like that,' he explained. 'I mean, she was only a whore. She likely got what was coming to her.'

I stood there in the centre of the room, no more than four feet away from him, and fought the impulse to slam him in the mouth. Keeping my voice low, I said, 'So you didn't dig too deeply into it?'

'The taxpayers don't *pay* me to dig too deeply into it,' he said. 'Not that kind of affair. Besides which, I got enough on my plate as it is.'

My eyes fell to the catalogue on the desk. 'Oh, I can see you're rushed off your feet,' I remarked softly.

'Look,' he snapped. 'We buried the girl at the county's expense. I don't see's how we could've done any more than that. 'Fact, if it'd been up to some of the councillors, she wouldn't even've got that much.'

The urge to strike out was stronger than ever now, but I knew I had to tread carefully. Any trouble I got myself into here would only delay me from taking off after Jay, and I was already four-going-on-five days behind him as it was.

'Got any idea where Bannon might've gone when he left town?' I asked.

He shook his head.

'Any ideas who might know?'

He frowned. 'What's your interest in alla this, anyhow?'

'That whore,' I said. 'She was my daughter, Torrance.'

His face went loose and his mouth dropped open. 'Hey now,' he said. 'I didn't mean no disrespects, mister, but ...' Suddenly he seemed to notice the gun on my hip, the cutaway holster, the fully-stocked shellbelt, and his expression hardened. 'You got a name, mister?'

'Allison.'

'Well, I'm sorry about your daughter, Mr Allison, but if you're thinking of going after Bannon, I'd advise against it.'

'Oh? And why would you do a thing like that?'

"Cause that'd be taking the law into your own

hands,' he replied firmly. 'And we don't allow that sorta thing no more, around here or anyplace else.'

'Jesus Christ, Torrance. My daughter was punched to death. Beaten till she just couldn't take it any more. What the hell else do you expect me to do, when the only kind of law I see around here is *your* kind?'

His eyes dropped away from my face.

I said, 'So long,' and made to turn away, but he came forward, put a hand on my arm and stopped me. I looked up at him, surprised to see genuine concern in his expression.

'Just watch your step around here, Allison,' he cautioned quietly. 'Jay Bannon had a lot of friends in this neck of the woods.'

'Including you?'

He shook his head. 'Bannon was a sonofabitch,' he replied savagely. 'And I'm not just saying that because of who you are and what he did. He was pure evil, that one—but popular with it.'

I nodded, pulled away from him and let myself out.

It was the middle of the morning and my stomach was telling me that even though I still didn't have much of an appetite, I'd better eat something. I walked further up the street, found an eats-house and went inside. I located a table, ordered food and then sat there, trying to work out in my mind just how in hell I was going to pick up Jay's cold trail.

The food came and I ate. It was all right, I guess. I really didn't think much about it. I paid my tab and went back out onto the street. I took out my pipe, stuffed it with rough-cut and fired it up. Again I thought about Nan. I knew I should wire her with the news, but I still didn't know how I was going to break it. I leaned against a porch upright and smoked and thought some more.

One thing was certain. To get answers, I first had to start asking questions. Even a chance remark made to one of these cronies of Jay's might provide the clue I needed.

I hit The Yellow Rose and six other saloons before I started to get the message. Sure, the bartenders, gamblers, percenters and owners, they all knew Jay. They knew what he'd done to his wife as well. But to them he was a swell fellow, always generous and good company. Even when they found out that his wife was my daughter, it made no difference. They were siding with their own, and I knew I'd get nothing out of them.

But still I kept trying. I heard a rumour that Jay had been figuring to head north. I found a solitaire-playing gamesman who'd heard something about him heading east to Louisiana.

And so it went on. I came out of the last saloon some time around two in the afternoon, feeling tired and frustrated but determined to carry on. I called into every gaming house I could find, every store, the stables, the Wells Fargo office, but everywhere I got pretty much the same result.

At last I drew to a halt on a street corner, feeling so mad that I could've chewed nails and spit rust. I'd lucked out at just about every place I'd been to. But I still had one last hope – the railroad depot.

I left the town behind me and followed the narrow, brushy roadway down to the station house. The day was still humid, and my shirt clung uncomfortably to the small of my back. A hundred yards down the line, a pall of dust hung high over the cattle pens as the cattle themselves milled aimlessly around their slat-sided pens. In the bushes to either side, birds hopped from twig to twig and filled the air with sweet songs. Inside my impractical boots, my feet were telling me that I'd never done so much walking in my life.

I entered the station house and went in search of the elderly agent, but he was nowhere to be seen. I walked out onto the warped platform, where the puddles had long since dried to ugly grey stains, but it was deserted. Cursing under my breath, I backtracked until I found his office and rapped on the door, but there was no answer. Taking a chance, I opened the door and peered inside. The small, cluttered room was dusty and lifeless.

I closed the door behind me and strode back through the building and out into the cleared yard, deciding to come back again later on.

Ouside, I hauled up sharp.

Three men were blocking my path. Three men who looked very much like hired toughs.

I ran my eyes over them in one swift pan. The first was tall and big-bellied, with a full blond-going-to-grey beard and a brown slouch hat covering long, straggly hair of much the same colour. There was a gunbelt fastened around the waistband of his grey duck pants, and he'd brushed his old corduroy coat back so that he could get to his Remington .44 quickly if he had to. He had blue eyes, a reddish, sweaty skin, a blob of pink putty for a nose and yellow, ragged teeth.

The man standing next to him was a little shorter, not so much fat as stocky, with the walnut grips of a Peacemaker projecting from the waistband of his Levis. He was of an age with his companion, I thought; dark-haired, square-jawed, bristly, with a pale scar down the left side of his face from his eyebrow to the corner of his mouth, and a black patch covering whatever was left of the eye itself.

At around five feet six, the third man was the shortest of the trio. He was skinny and weasel-faced, with brown eyes and a long, sharp nose. He was dressed in a faded, repaired claw-hammer jacket and striped California pants, and he wore an old gibus hat perched at a cocky angle on his slick, fair hair. He carried no gun that I could see, but somehow I didn't expect him to. No; this fellow had the look of a knifeman about him.

I held my ground for a moment more. Then, when it became obvious that they weren't going to get out of my way I said, sociably enough, 'Help you fellers?'

It was the short one who answered, and he had to speak around a cool, cock-sure grin to do it. 'Understan' you been askin' after Jay Bannon, Allison.'

There was no need to deny it. I nodded. 'You know him?'

'Uh-huh.'

'Can you tell me where I can find him?'

'Nuh-huh.'

'Well, maybe you can tell me why you've come searching me out.'

'You've been askin' after Jay,' Shorty said again. 'We don't like that.' He glanced at his two companions, and they nodded their agreement. 'So happens Jay's a friend of ours.'

Now I knew for sure that they were here to make trouble. In the distance cattle bawled, and a warm breeze fanned our faces and filtered through our hair.

'I guess that kind of puts us on opposite sides of the fence, huh?' I said.

Shorty cackled at the understatement. 'That's one waya puttin' it,' he agreed. 'That's why we're gon' give you some advice I jus' *know* you're gon' take.' His eyes went flat and he said, 'Go on home, Allison. Go on home an' forget all about what happened to your daughter. She was just a slut anyway, not worth gettin' hurt over. But you keep on comin' an' I swear we'll break you in two.'

He was trying to goad and anger me, because angry men are usually careless men as well. I wasn't going to fall for it, but even so, my voice was low and throaty when I said, 'All right, Shorty. You've said *your* piece. Now I'll say *mine*. If you fellers know where Bannon's gone, you'd better tell me fast. If not, you better get the hell out of my way and let me pass, 'cause either way I'm coming through, and you'd better believe that I'm going to stick after Jay till I find him.'

Shorty shook his head in disapproval. 'Well,' he sighed regretfully, 'I'll say this for you, dad. You sure talk a good fight.'

'I do more than talk it,' I replied, and because there was three of them and only one of me, I got in first and took the lot of them by surprise.

Pivoting, I kicked the fat man in the left kneecap, and while he was howling and jumping around on one leg, I hurled myself at the man next to him, Eye-Patch. We smashed into each other and he loosed off a startled yell as we both went down in a tangle, luckily with me on top.

We crashed to the dirt and I punched him all over to weaken and distract him. We rolled over, still kicking and punching, with dust clouds smoking up around us, and I heard Shorty screeching, '*Grab him, Billy! Hold him!*'

Eye-Patch — Billy — started trying to do exactly that.

I punched him some more, in the face, on top of his head once his hat fell off, anywhere I thought I could hurt him, and he did the same to me because that's what fighting is all about. I punched him so hard that my knuckles split, but I paid them no mind. I could spare some time for hurting later, but not now.

Once I figured I'd inflicted enough damage on him, at least for the time being, I threw myself sideways and crabbed away from him. I got a fleeting glimpse at his face — he was bleeding from one nostril and his right eye was puffing up and turning blue. Then I came back up onto my feet and collided with Shorty, who was coming at me with a long, thin blade sparkling in one hand.

He took a wild swipe at me and instinctively I leapt backwards, out of reach of the blade. I saw by the way he handled the knife that he'd had considerable experience with it. You could tell by the way he held it, the way he kept trying to distract me with the snakelike contortions of his other hand.

He came in again, moving fast, and I thought I felt the blade cut through the material of my shirt.

After that we fell apart and circled warily for a moment, sweating hard, breathing hard, each of us trying to get the measure of the other. A few yards away, Billy was crawling around on his hands and knees, practically blind now that his one good eye had puffed shut, and the fat man was still hopping up and down and holding his damaged leg.

Then, all at once, Shorty yelled something about me being a God-damn sonofabitch and came at me in a stabbing rush I just couldn't hope to dodge. It was the last thing I'd been expecting him to do, and I had to think fast to counter him. I twisted my body sideways and let him push the knife at the empty space between my right arm and my right side. Then, before he could pull back, I brought my arm back in, so that I had his wrist clamped against my body.

There was a pause of maybe two seconds then. A look of horror distorted his face, because all of a sudden he knew that I had him, and that I was going to hurt him.

I did.

I tightened my hold on him and twisted hard and fast, and he screamed because I'd just broken his wrist. I let him go and danced back away from him, but I needn't have worried; Shorty was now the least of my worries. He dropped the knife and sank down onto his knees, cradling the shattered joint. I kicked the knife away from him and it skittered into some long grass like a stiff silver snake.

But there was no time for me to regain my breath. The fat man was all through hopping and howling, and now he was out for blood. He'd drawn and cocked his Remington and I threw myself groundward even as he fired it at me.

I jarred against the earth, half-choked as the breath knocked out of me, then powered back up, launched myself at him and grabbed hold of his gunhand by the wrist.

He growled at me and tried to claw my eyes out with his free hand while he struggled to cock the Remington again. I felt the barrel of the gun pressing into my stomach and somewhere deep inside my head I prayed to God that he wouldn't pull the trigger a second time.

In desperation I hit him in the belly but my fist bounced off, so I stamped on one of his big feet instead and he started howling all over again. Taking advantage of his sudden confusion, I twisted his wrist and he spun around and before he properly knew what was happening, I had his gunarm jammed halfway up his back.

He howled as I shouted at him to drop the gun, but something somewhere went badly wrong and he tightened his finger on the trigger instead. In the next moment a shot rang out and he stiffened as his chest erupted in a violent burst of blood and meat.

I realised that he'd gone and back-shot himself and I thought, *Aw, you stupid sonuver* –

Then I threw him away and he fell down as if there wasn't a bone left in him.

But it *still* wasn't over.

Ten feet away Billy was back on his feet, his .45 in his hand. I saw it buck in his fist, heard it add to the thunder still ringing in my ears from the fat man's blast, saw blue-grey smoke drift sideways, away from the short barrel. Then I heard the bullet spang off the front of the station house and I thanked my lucky stars that his vision was still impaired.

Before he could make his second shot count, my

right hand blurred across my body, folded around the hard rubber grips of my Army Colt and dragged it free with a leathery whisper.

Billy called me a dirty Indian dog and jabbed his Peacemaker at me again. My own Colt came up. I cocked, aimed and fired, and something destructive happened to Billy's right shoulder, it made a *splat* kind of sound and blood exploded from it in a crimson shower. He fell sideways and wailed like a banshee, then rocked backwards and forwards on the ground and screamed for a doctor.

It was done now, the violence, and it left me trembling with reaction. I looked at Shorty, bending forward as if in prayer, clutching his broken wrist as if he thought his hand might fall off; at Billy, trying desperately to stem the flow of blood from his shoulder, his stocky frame shaking as he sobbed; at the fat man, spread-eagled on the ground, soaked in blood and as dead as a dinosaur. It wasn't a sight that a man could take any pride in, but these men had brought it all on themselves, and I couldn't find any sympathy for them, either.

Suddenly I heard a sound behind me and I spun around with my Colt streaking up. Framed in the station house doorway was the elderly agent, his face as white as chalk. From the look of his half-fastened trousers, he'd been visiting the out-house while all of this had been happening.

Staring wide-eyed down the barrel of my gun, he said, 'Jeezus Christ, mister, d-don't shoot!'

I put the gun up and he dropped his shoulders, finally turning his attention to what was left of Jay's three friends. 'Christ Almighty,' he breathed.

'What's been happening here?'

'You better go and fetch the marshal,' I said by way of reply. 'A doctor too, if you've got one.'

He bobbed his head eagerly, probably glad of the excuse to get out of there. 'I'm on my way,' he said, and broke into a waddling kind of trot.

I felt hot and tired. I was aching where I'd been hit and feeling shaky where I'd nearly been shot. But when my eyes found Shorty again, I knew this thing wasn't over yet. There were still questions to be asked ... and answers to get.

FOUR

I went over and knelt beside Shorty, then grabbed him by the shoulder and shook him hard to get his attention. He moaned and begged me to stop. I did, and jammed my Colt into his screwed-up, sweat-slimy face instead.

'Bannon,' I grated. 'Where is he?'

He shook his head, and his words came out in a confused jumble. 'I don't know! I swear it! Allison, we jus' thought – '

I cocked the Colt and the hammer made a ratchety *cli-cli-click* that made his slightly glazed eyes widen. '*Where is he, you little bastard!*'

'Don't tell 'im!' yelled Billy, biting down on the pain of his ruined shoulder.

Shorty said, 'I swear to God – '

'God's not here,' I told him, taking up the first pressure on the trigger and making sure that he saw me do it. 'But I *am*.'

Spittle flecked his lips as he babbled desperately. 'Aw cris', you ain't gon' shoot me! We didn't mean you no harm, we w-wuz only funnin', that's all. F-fer God's sake, Allison …!'

Behind me, Billy's voice rose to a roar. 'He's bluffin', Finn!'

I could feel the dead flatness of my eyes as they

bored into him. 'Am I, Shorty?' I asked. My finger tightened some more. 'Where'd he go, the feller who killed my daughter?'

Billy shouted, 'Don't tell 'im! He's bluffin', I tell ya!'

My finger tightened just a fraction more.

Shorty broke then. He saw something in my look that convinced him that I *wasn't* bluffing and brought his good hand up to try and ward me off. '*All right!*' he sobbed. 'All right, I'll *tell* you! Jus ... put that goddam gun down!'

I didn't put the gun down, I pointed it skywards and said, 'I'm listening.'

'Finn – !'

Stalling, Shorty – Finn – said, 'Aw God, you gotta get me to a doctor ...'

'In a minute. Maybe. I want to hear about Bannon first. Where'd he go when he lit out Saturday night?'

He was trembling now. Hunching up and taking hold of his loose wrist again, he muttered, 'Oklahoma Station.'

I frowned. 'What'd you say?'

'*Damn you, Finn!*'

'Oklahoma Station,' he repeated.

I'd never heard of the place, but I reckoned I'd have time to find out its exact whereabouts later. 'What's he doing up there?' I asked.

He gave a careful shrug. 'S-somethin' t'do with the Land Rush'd be my guess. Y-yeah, that'd be it. H-he'd been sayin' as how he wuz gon' make a killin' up at Oklahoma Station, what with all them know-nothin' rubes up there, jus' waitin' to be suckered.'

'You're sure about that?'

'S-sure ...'

'If you're lying to me, you worthless little bastard ...' I brought the gun down again.

'I swear to God it's the truth!' he whined desperately.

I straightened up and thought about what he'd said. The Land Rush, what they were already calling "The Rush of '89" ... I'd heard about it. The Government had bought two million acres of unassigned land bang in the middle of Indian Territory and were going to open it up to would-be homesteaders sometime within the next month. But because the demand was expected to be so great, it had been decided that the land should be apportioned on a first come, first served basis. Thus, at noon on April 22nd, every settler would have to race all the others into the unassigned lands if he were to get his hundred-sixty acres. There were going to be a lot of winners, it was true ... But inevitably there were going to be a lot of losers as well, for I'd heard rumours that the Land Rush was already drawing possible homesteaders like a magnet, tens of thousands of them.

The more I thought about it, the more I could see that it was just the kind of place Jay *would* head for. With a woman-killing on his hands, he'd be looking to lose himself in a crowd. And deep down he was so damned greedy that he'd be hard put to resist the easy pickings to be had among all those 'know-nothing rubes' at Oklahoma Station.

I nodded to myself, convinced that Shorty was telling the truth. That's where Jay had gone, all right.

It was where I would go.

* * *

It was about five-thirty, heading towards six, when I finally let myself back into the shack. Even as I was closing the door behind me, Connie was hurrying across the room towards me, her dark eyes ranging critically over my face, neck and shoulders, torso, searching for wounds.

'My God, Mr Allison,' she said. 'I've been going out of my mind! Is it true what I've been hearing? That you killed a man and wounded two others? Are you hurt?'

I shook my head. 'I'm fine.'

'Your lip's swollen, and there's a bump on your forehead.'

'They'll heal.'

She looked at me for a moment more, then nodded. 'I guess,' she allowed. 'You look done in, though. Go sit down and I'll fetch you some coffee, heat some water so you can wash your face.'

She turned away and headed for the range. I said, 'Jay's gone north, Connie. To Oklahoma Station.'

She stopped what she was doing and turned to face me. When she spoke her voice was a murmur. 'Are you sure?'

I nodded.

I was aching from the punishment I'd dished out and taken, and tired, too. I'd had to go through everything that had happened three times before Marshal Torrance was satisfied that I'd done what I had in self-defence, and even then he'd warned me not to leave town because I would have to repeat everything I'd said for the benefit of the county coroner.

'To hell with that,' I'd snapped irritably. 'I've already told you, Torrance. I haven't got the time for any of that. I'm pulling out tomorrow.'

He raised his hands, palms outward, to silence me. 'I know, I know,' he cut in. 'You want to get after Bannon. But your private little war's gonna have to wait, Allison. We got to observe due process, here.'

'Like you did with my Clare?' I shot back. 'I didn't see any regard for the law where *she* was concerned.'

We argued some more after that, but eventually he sighed and allowed as how a sworn statement duly signed and witnessed should satisfy the coroner's court.

Now Connie turned back to the range and continued to fix the coffee. I watched her as the coming sunset leeched the light from the shack and my grandson crawled around on the floor, his palms making little slapping noises on the boards, his knees shuffling as he crawled towards me and began to inspect my boots.

Finally I said, 'Connie, about the boy …'

Without turning around again she cut in, 'I'm not taking the responsibility of him, Mr … uh, Jim. I've done it up to now because there's been no-one else, but –'

'I can't take him with me,' I said simply. 'You *know* I can't.'

'Well, *I* can't look after him,' she replied. 'Not the way he ought to be looked after, I mean. I've got a living to earn.'

I bent down and picked him up, then walked over to her. 'Connie,' I said, and though I tried not to beg, that's the way it came out. 'You've got to help me. If I don't take off after Jay first thing tomorrow, I might *never* catch him.'

This time she *did* look at me. Then her eyelashes came down and she shook her head.

'All right,' I said. 'You've got a living to earn. I understand that. So let me *hire* you to take the baby home for me, to my place along the Gila. I'll pay you for your trouble. I'll pay you well.'

'But I couldn't just up and leave Wetherby ...'

'Why not? What's here to stop you?' I countered. 'Look, I know I'm asking a lot, but I'm desperate, girl, and if you want the truth, I'm not willing to trust my grandson with anyone else. Besides, how long do you think you can keep going in this line, singing for a bunch of deadbeats who don't even know you're *there* half the time? How much longer do you *want* to keep going?'

I saw pain stir in her eyes. 'You're a nice man and I like you a lot, Mr Allison,' she said stiffly. 'But don't you think you're getting a mite personal?'

I guessed I was. 'All right, Connie. I'm sorry.'

I ran my hand up through my hair. There seemed to be no option but to take the boy with me, but Judas Priest – a boy not yet three-quarters of a year old, riding with his granpaw on a killing mission ... it made me feel sick just to think about it.

I washed up and drank some coffee, and then I told Connie that I had to go back down to the railroad depot and find out how I was going to get to Oklahoma Station. As I pulled my hat on, I told her she could sleep in her own bed tonight, because I'd find somewhere else. It was about the most I'd said since she'd turned me down.

'There's no need for that,' she replied. 'I can

share with one of the other girls at the Yellow Rose. One more night won't hurt me.'

I nodded. 'Thanks.'

I went back down to the depot and spent some time picking the old station agent's brain. As luck would have it, Indian Territory was well served by the railroads, and Oklahoma Station actually turned out to be a stop on the Atchison, Topeka and Santa Fe line. The station agent, still leery of me, assured me that a northbound connection with the Missouri, Kansas and Texas Railroad would take me pretty much where I wanted to go.

On the way back to the shack I stopped by a saloon and brought myself a whiskey. I was finally starting to get somewhere. But I still had to tell Nan about Clare. Eventually I decided to put everything down in a letter and mail it and a covering note to Doc Miller, a good family friend in Lordsburg. It was a hell of a thing to ask of another man, but I figured it would be better if Nan heard the news from a friend. After that doc could give her my note, which would explain everything – including what I intended to do about it – in more deatil.

I left the saloon and hurried back through the darkness, anxious to write my letters and have done with it. When I let myself into the shack, Connie Crane was sitting in a chair facing the door, the baby snuggled up on her lap.

I looked at her in some surprise. 'Shouldn't you be at work?' I asked curiously.

She smiled gently. 'I quit,' she replied. 'I told them I just picked up another job. In New Mexico.'

I blinked at her, almost unable to believe my ears. 'You … you mean you'll do it?' I asked carefully. 'You'll take James home for me?'

'Yes, Mr … Jim,' she said. 'All I ask is one thing.'
'Name it.'

She said flatly, 'When you catch up with Jay, put a bullet in him for me.'

I nodded. 'You've got it, Connie,' I promised grimly. 'You've got it.'

With Connie and the baby headed for New Mexico and my letters to Doc Miller safely in the mail, I set out on my own trek north later the following day. It took me a week and a half to reach Oklahoma Station, which was about four hundred miles from Wetherby. I would have made it sooner but for the fact that the nearer I got to my destination, the slower I was forced to go.

At first the train journey passed like any other. My mind busy with other thoughts, I paid it little notice. But the further north we steamed, the more crowded the train became, and every time we reached another stop there were more potential homesteaders waiting to squeeze themselves aboard.

It seemed like half of America was intent on making for the unassigned lands. I'd never seen so many people all headed for one place, and to see it now was a little scary. Two million acres up for grabs sounded a lot, but I knew that even a quarter of the people I saw would be lucky to actually stake their claims.

Inevitably delays occurred, sometimes long ones, and as tempers frayed fights and arguments broke out. Soon there were so many people and possessions aboard that the train could only crawl sluggishly on across the endless, treeless flats.

At Paducah I lost patience with the slow progress and tried to find a quicker means of transport. But even there it was much the same story. You couldn't get close to the Wells Fargo office for people who all had the same idea as me. In the end I found a livery and bought a reddish-brown California sorrel and a second-hand saddle, and struck out on my own.

It was a bad move. All the trails I sought out were choked with would-be settlers and their heavy-laden wagons. Mostly I saw raggedy-assed men in tall boots, walking along beside lumbering wagons and teams of oxen, everything they had in the world — including their wives and apparently endless families – crammed in the backs.

I spotted Conestogas, wagonettes, Dougherty wagons, celerity wagons, babouches and even bob-sleighs. I saw ambitious young men riding horses and bicycles. I saw optimistic young newlyweds and prematurely-aged farmers from the dustbowls of Kansas, all hoping to find a new life. I even saw a few old-timers who must've known they wouldn't stand a chance when the starting pistol was fired and the race was finally on.

I skirted round as much of them as I could and kept my horse pointed north and a little east. Eventually low hills shoved up in the distance, as did scrub oak and hickory. The soil turned rich and red, and short, wiry buffalo and grama grass formed a carpet under my sorrel's thundering hooves. I was in Indian Territory now.

Three hard days later I reached the end of the trail.

From a distance, Oklahoma Station was an unending sea of canvas, tent after tent, wagon after wagon, all fanning out from the few weathered board buildings of the station itself, and beyond the glistening ribbons of the railroad tracks lay the rolling plains that these tens of thousands of hopefuls had come to claim – a land slashed by ravines and gullies, stippled with redbud, maple, dogwood and pecan, scored with creeks and rivers and bumped with low, gypsum-crowned hills, mild in winter, scorching in summer. What they were already calling The District.

I slowed my horse with a gentle tug on the reins and entered the tent city at a walk.

Adults, children and livestock were everywhere. Tents had been set up with no regard for order, and wagons had been parked wherever their owners had seen fit to unhitch and quarter their oxen. One or two patriots had hung the Stars and Stripes outside their bivouacs. Others had said to hell with that, and just gone ahead and opened big tent saloons to cater for an endless procession of thirsty men instead.

As I rode deeper, I saw at least five open-air emporiums selling everything the potential settler would be likely to need when the time finally came to set up house. Enterprising attorneys and agents for the US Land Office conducted their business from behind simple wooden crates. Around them, oblivious to all the noise and confusion, horses and goats grazed contentedly, while chickens strutted here and there and hogs snuffled at any likely looking piles of garbage in search of swill.

The whole place had a picnic atmosphere to it. Blanket-draped Cherokee and Seminole Indians watched the gathering of the white men with bitter bemusement. I rode deeper into the throng, keeping watchful just in case I should touch lucky and spot Jay at once. It was vital that I remain vigilant, because he would be wary and expecting pursuit. He knew me well enough to know that once I found out what he'd done to Clare, I wouldn't let up until I found him and made him pay.

But every place I looked there were so many faces that I began to realise that I'd badly underestimated just how difficult my quest was going to be.

It was about then that someone behind me suddenly yelled, '*Out of the way, there! Coming through!*' and the next thing I knew, a detachment of blue-clad cavalrymen were bearing down on me, and scattering homesteaders in their path.

Quickly I yanked my horse over to the side of the crooked, makeshift road as they surged past. For several seconds there was only a blur of movement, rising dust, the jangle of harness and accoutrements … and then they were gone.

In my immediate area several children, distressed by the soldiers' sudden appearance, had started crying. I sat my saddle, hands folded around the horn, and watched as the troopers clattered madly up and over the railroad tracks three hundred yards away and then galloped on across what was still technically no man's land.

Homesteader men drifted back into what passed for a street, muttering sourly about the soldiers and speculating on the nature of their sortie into The District. Puzzled by a mention of 'more damn' sooners', I dismounted and asked a brawny, red-faced man in farmer's breeches and brogans what he meant. He looked at me as if the answer should be obvious, but then went on to explain that while most of the homesteaders were willing to hold back and take their chances at noon on the 22nd — now no more than a week away — there were others who were constantly trying to slip quietly into The District and stake their claims ahead of everyone else. These, he said, were the 'sooners'. A detachment of the Fifth Cavalry's F Troop had been sent up from Fort Reno to make sure that anyone attempting to literally 'jump the gun' didn't get away with it. But, as he pointed out, it was going on all the time.

'An' is it any wonder, when you've got men ever'where you look tellin' you they know the best way to get into The District undetected, an' offerin' to smuggle you in for a price?' he complained, spitting to one side in a gesture of disgust.

It was late afternoon and the day was muggy. Again I took a look around. A train whistle shrilled through the close air, signalling the arrival of yet another settler-crammed string of carriages.

I shook my head, disheartened by the near-impossibility of my task, and checked the time. It was too late to do much of anything now except find a place to wash up, buy a meal at one of a dozen tent restaurants and then locate a spot to make camp. My search for Jay would have to begin tomorrow.

That night I camped in a shady hollow on the easternmost fringe of the sprawling tent city and thought about home. By now Nan would have received her visit from Doc Miller. She'd know that our daughter was dead, and that I had come after her killer. And Connie should have reached the ranch by this time. I thought about James, and wondered what Nan would make of him.

I turned in early and threw back my blankets much the same way at sun-up next morning. I had no real plan of action to follow. It would be much as it had been in Wetherby, just a lot of leg-work and questions and hope.

By my estimate there were about thirty or forty thousand people in the temporary town. Although the ones I questioned were willing enough to offer whatever help they could, they'd never heard of the man I described to them, and neither did his name strike them as familiar. To make the job more difficult, new people were arriving in their hundreds practically every hour of the day. I couldn't hope to question them all.

The sun was setting on my third fruitless day at Oklahoma Station when I decided to buy myself some supper and then turn in down at my secluded campsite away to the east. Settlers were starting to light lanterns and canvas was taking on a pleasing cast. Surrounded as I was by so many families, I couldn't help but feel lonely out there. Neither did my reason for being there offer any cheer.

On impulse I decided to stop by one of the temporary saloons and have a couple of drinks before bedding down. The company would do me good, and I might stand more chance of finding someone who'd seen or knew Jay in such a place. I changed course and headed for an area where most of the tent saloons had congregated.

It was as I was approaching one such drinking parlour that my attention was suddenly taken by a string of panicky yells.

'*Help me, somebody! For God's sake, they're killin' 'im!*'

About thirty yards ahead, a gangling boy of about thirteen had burst out of a narrow dogtrot between one saloon tent and the next, freckled, tow-headed and scared half to death. Again he screamed, '*Please! Somebody!*'

A few homesteader men were working nearby, and three of them went over to the boy, their faces illuminated by the flickering storm lanterns that hung from poles outside each of the saloons.

'All right, son,' said one. 'Calm down, now. What's the problem?'

'It's my pa!' the boy shrieked, mingled fear and concern yanking his fevered face all out of shape. 'They're *killin'* 'im back there!'

The homesteader reached out to put his hand on his arm. 'Come, now ...'

The boy shrugged out of his grip, his fists clenched at his sides. 'They're *killin'* 'im, I tell ya! He was playin' cards in that there saloon an' when he found out they was cheatin' 'im, he told 'em to give him his money back, but they took him out the back instead, an' now, awjeez, they're killin' 'im!'

The homesteader looked over the boy's head, into the shadowy dogtrot, but he seemed reluctant to go and see for himself. I couldn't blame him, not entirely. He was a farmer, not a fighter. He likely had his own family to consider. But one look at the anguish on the kid's face was enough for me. I guess I'd been a lawman for so long that at this late date it was in my blood.

I pushed through the small crowd that had gathered and said, 'Where is he, son? Your pa?'

Relief washed over the kid's freckled face and it was pitiful to see. He jabbed a finger down the muddy alleyway. 'Out the back!' he screeched, trembling. 'Aw God, it's terrible what they're doin' to 'im! You gotta come an' help 'im!'

I put a hand on his arm and squeezed. 'Stay here.'

The homesteaders had been fixing a busted wagon wheel on the other side of the narrow strip of roadway. I went over and helped myself to a stout spoke from the shattered wheel they'd been in the process of replacing, then hustled down the dogtrot feeling taut in the stomach.

I heard them now, the regular, sodden thud of connecting punches, the sharp groans and gasps of the man taking them. I moved faster, my shadow thrown large against the canvas beside me, and a moment later I was there.

The cleared area behind the big, patched tent had been set up pretty much like a backyard, with three heavy Conestoga wagons forming a rough perimeter fifty feet square. Wooden crates and iron-strapped barrels were stacked everywhere, and more of the same were lashed down tight beneath olive green tarpaulins. The yard was a mess – the grass had been churned to a kind of dried mud, and spare tables and chairs had been piled into an untidy heap on the far side. A lantern had been balanced atop a low stack of kegs, so that the two men who were beating the boy's father could see what they were doing.

One of them was holding the farmer erect while the other was hitting him in the belly. They dwarfed their victim, the pair of them; hell, they dwarfed *me*, and I'm big enough.

Putting some of the old authority back into my voice I snapped, 'All right, break it up!'

The feller doing all the hitting turned on his heel and looked at me. His eyes dropped to my chest first, to see if I was wearing a badge. He was in his mid-twenties, a thick-set six-footer, with great, corded muscles knotting and bunching in his exposed arms, and a thick neck. He had a vicious look to him that was heightened by the fact that he'd obviously been enjoying his work until I'd interrupted him. He'd worked up a light sheen of sweat and now he brought one massive arm up to wipe it out of his clear blue eyes.

'An' who the hell're you?' he growled. He had just the kind of voice you'd expect a man like him to have, like one stone slab sliding across another.

Ignoring him, I addressed myself to his equally big partner, who was standing behind the farmer, holding him erect. 'Let him go.'

This one was older, about forty, with stubble for hair, a matching set of cauliflower ears and a broken nose. He cracked a snarl at me and I saw that his teeth were gappy and chipped. His eyes were piercing and brown, his lumpy face the face of a man who loved a rough-house the way other men loved a drink or a gamble or a woman.

'This ain't none of your business,' he said. 'Was I you, I'd butt out.'

I looked at the farmer in his grasp. What I saw there made me wince. He was unconscious, and his face was smudged blue and red. They'd done a good, thorough job on him, and they weren't finished yet. But any more and it would go from a beating to murder.

'Let him go,' I said again, more impatiently this time.

The first of the plug-uglies said over his

shoulder, 'You stay right where you are, Cal.' Then he advanced towards me.

I let him come, and when he was near enough I brought the wheel-spoke up and smashed him right in the side of the face with it. He shuddered and said, '*Uhhhh …*' and then his eyes rolled up into his head and he fell over sideways.

'Let him go,' I said to Cal, speaking through clenched teeth now. 'Less you want some of the same.'

Cal glared at me, breathing hard and fast, letting his fury build. To our right, someone pushed the rear tent flap aside and a knot of curious, liquored-up homesteaders plugged the gap.

At last Cal let go of the farmer and stepped over him when he crumpled to the ground. He was tall and stocky, dressed in a collarless white shirt and high-waisted grey pants held up by a wide leather belt. Like all big men, he moved in a lumbering, cumbersome kind of fashion. He came at me in a rush and I used the wheel-spoke again, but this time he saw it coming and put up one hand to block my swing, and when the wheel-spoke struck him on the bare right arm it snapped, and all at once I was left only with a useless splinter.

I thought, *Hell* –

– and then he was right there in front of me, swinging a hard right fist straight for my jaw.

Dropping what was left of the wheel-spoke, I back-pedalled fast, but not quite fast enough. He caught me in the face and lights popped inside my skull, but because I was moving away from him the blow didn't connect with as much force as it might have, and that was lucky for me.

He came after me, his shadow and mine leaping

all over the stalled Conestogas, and the men in the
tent flap began to roar their excitement. I blocked
a left cross, ducked a right. His fist went sweeping
over my head and slammed into one of the stacked
barrels. Dark beer rushed out in a gulping torrent
and some of the watching men laughed. That only
enraged Cal more, and when he ripped his hand
free of the splintery slats he pulled the barrel away
with him and the thing shattered to matchwood at
his feet.

He came at me again. I hit him. He hit me. I felt
his blow, but I doubt that he felt mine. We circled,
feinted, danced back and clashed again. I didn't
want to fight him. We were so unevenly matched
that I didn't stand a chance. I knew that all I had to
do to finish it was draw my Colt, but dammit he was
unarmed, and I'm kind of stupid like that.

He rushed me again, and suddenly I was backing
up fast. The watchers howled their delight. I
stumbled over something – the plug-ugly I'd
knocked out – and in that second Cal had me in his
great paws and I knew that I was finished.

FIVE

He grabbed me in a bear-hug and lifted me off the ground. Then he started to squeeze the wind right out of me and my face twisted up as I fought to loosen the crushing grip.

He swung me around and tightened his hold still further, and I started kicking my legs like a man having a fit, hoping that it would unbalance him and make him loosen his grip. But he just gave another jerk that seemed to wring out what little air still remained in my lungs, and I screwed my eyes shut and started gasping for breath all over again.

Beads of sweat the size of pearls popped on my forehead and dribbled down my contorted face. It was like I was caught in a band of iron that was getting tighter all the time.

He tightened his hold one more notch. I could feel the hard knots of his thumbs and fingers in my back. Each of his hands was locked around the other arm, and he was slowly, relentlessly working them along until they could close around the elbows.

Blood was pounding in my ears. I felt every pulse in my body thudding fit to explode. Something strained in my side and I hoped to God it wasn't a rib splintering.

I forced my eyelids back and looked into my opponent's face. He was sweating too, with the effort it was taking to press me into death or unconsciousness. *Damn you*, I thought. *Still, if that's what you want …*

Without warning I went limp in his grip, and instinctively he let up on some of the pressure because he thought I'd gone to someplace where pain could no longer touch me. But he was wrong. The minute I sensed that he'd lowered his guard, I brought my head forward, right into his face, and my forehead connected hard with his nose.

It flattened like a wet sponge and Cal bellowed something incoherent. He let go of me and staggered backwards, both hands going to his levelled nose, and I fell away from him and sucked in a deep breath. Lights were still popping in front of my face and I shook my head to clear them away. About five feet ahead, Cal was roaring something and shaking himself the way a wet dog shakes himself when he wants to get dry. In the lamplight I saw thick gobbets of blood arc into the air from his ruined nose.

I threw myself at him, pummelled him mercilessly in the belly with a right-left-right combination that got the suddenly-hushed spectators yelling again, then turned my attention to his face, and more specifically, his well-defined jaw.

I punched him one, two, three, then he started blocking me and trying to hit back. I blocked what I could and ducked beneath the rest, then started going for his body again, hitting him all over, taking a wild kind of satisfaction from every grunt and cry he gave.

He hit me a clubbing blow to the side of the head

and the lights came popping back before my eyes, but I wasn't through yet, I was going to finish this big, vicious bastard any way I could, because the alternative didn't bear thinking about.

I kicked him twice in the shin and while he was roaring at the pain of that I hit him some more in the stomach. My hands were aching, my wrists were aching, but still I kept jabbing away at him. He was weakening, you could tell by the way he was stumbling around the yard after me.

I snatched up a heavy crate and threw it at him. He tried to check it but it and the bottles in it shattered against his upraised arms and showered him in wood and whiskey.

Now his guard had dropped and I had my pick of his face or his belly. I went for both; I hit him right in the blood-soaked face and quick as a flash hit him again in the stomach. He bent forward and I used my knee on him this time, I brought it up and caught him bang in the face, and he straightened back up and suddenly the yard went absolutely silent again.

Cal stood there on slightly spread legs, looking down at me through glazed eyes. I looked back at him, wary, expecting a trap. But still he just stood there, swaying gently, arms hanging limp at his sides.

Cautiously I reached out one hand, put it on his broad chest and shoved.

He keeled over backwards.

The cheer that rose up from the saloon's patrons nearly deafened me. I stood over him, the victor, but there was no sense of triumph in me. Victory wasn't what this had been about. I'd wanted no part in it, I'd merely reacted to the situation as it turned out. All I wanted now was to soak my hands in a saline solution and go to sleep and then go back to trying to find Jay tomorrow morning.

But the spectators had other ideas. All at once I was surrounded by them, and they were slapping me on the back, unaware of the agony they were sending through my tender muscles. I stood there, drawing in deep draughts of air, wanting only to get away from it all.

'Come on, mister, buy you a drink!' yelled one enthusiastic sport.

'Yeah, come on, mister, I bet you could use it!'

'Hell, you sure 'nuff earned it!'

I scanned the crowd for the farmer Cal and his buddy had been beating up. I caught sight of him on the outer fringe of the mob. He was stooped over, blotting his bloody face with a kerchief, and his boy was beside him, clinging to one of his arms, tears showing hot and salty on his cheeks.

I felt sick. That was reaction setting in. I closed my eyes and tried to fight it off. That other feller had been right – I *could* use a drink. But more than that I just wanted to crawl away somewhere quiet and lick my wounds.

I felt them pulling me towards the tent and I opened my eyes again so that I could see where I was going. It was then that I saw him, standing no more than seven or eight feet away from me, towards the back of the crowd, and suddenly I froze in my tracks because, God help me –

– it was *Jay Bannon*.

For a moment I was rooted to the spot, unable to grasp that it really *was* him. I was wrong. I *had* to be. But that mop of curly blue-black hair, those penetrating brown eyes, that long nose, wide mouth –

Dammit, it *was* him!

I opened my mouth and muttered something. I don't recall what it was. Then I pulled away from the men who were trying to urge me into the tent and made a lunge for him, and the cry that came out of me was something primeval.

'*BAANNNNONNNN!*'

My hands came up to grab him, and the look of horror that had frozen his face suddenly thawed and he pitched drunkenly around and swiftly waded through the jostling crowd.

I went after him, still bellowing his name, but the rest of them held me back. I guess they thought I'd gone a little crazy during the fight because they kept telling me to calm down, that it was all behind me now.

Again I tried to pull myself free of them, galvanised into fresh action by the sight of the man I had come here to kill, and no longer aware of the aches and pains racking my face, arms, hands and body.

But then someone beside me spoke closely to my ear. 'What's a matter, Jim – don't you wanna sample the finest blackstrap in Oklahoma Station?'

I very nearly ignored him. All I was interested in right then was Bannon. But dimly I recognised something familiar in the voice, something that warned me to be on my guard, and reluctantly I broke stride. As much as I wanted to go after Jay – and Lord, how I wanted to go after him – I knew I'd better watch my back, if the speaker was who I thought he was.

I turned around and yeah, it was him all right –
Edgar Vallance.

Sharp Edgar Vallance ... God, I'd never thought
to lay my eyes on that sonofabitch again. He'd been
a whiskey pedlar back in the old days, one of the
worst. He knew the Indians loved to drink, and
knew equally well that alcohol was forbidden in the
Territory, but still he brewed his foul concoction
up at his place in the Ouachita Mountains and then
ferried it down over the line in a string of wagons
and sold keg after keg of it in every Indian
settlement he came to. Creek, Cherokee, Choctaw,
Seminole ... they were all the same to Ed Vallance.
He sold his whiskey wherever and whenever he
could, then cleared out fast so that he never got to
see any of the trouble it caused. And *what* trouble;
fights, robberies, killings ...

The Cherokee Light Horse had tried to catch
him and did, but he bribed his way out of trouble
on three seperate occasions. When he sold some
bad stuff that killed seven Chickasaws, Judge
Parker decided that enough was enough and sent
me into the Nations to find him and fetch him
back.

Sharp Edgar Vallance. The man with his eye
always on the main chance. When he'd heard that I
was on his trail he'd sent one of his men back to
ambush me. That was in the spring of '83. I lost a
good horse in the fight, and was lucky to escape
with my life, unlike the other party. But Ed always
managed to stay one jump ahead of me, and I
never did get to collar him and bring him in to
stand before the judge.

Now he nodded to me. 'Hello, Jim.' He was a
short, rotund man of six and fifty summers, with a

jowly, whiskery face, a big, round, pitted nose and loose lips. His head was as smooth as an egg but some greasy black hair still lingered above his ears and at the base of his skull. He was dressed in a stained white shirt and his grey wool pants were held up by wide black suspenders. He wore his pants shoved into cracked knee-boots, and carried a big Smith & Wesson .44 in a holster on one fleshy hip. To look at him you'd think he was soft and genial but he wasn't; he was cold and hard, like granite. Believe me, I *know*.

It had gone quiet around us, as the home-steaders began to sense the enmity between us, but eventually I returned the nod. "Ed. Still plying the same dirty trade, I see.'

He gestured to the absence of a badge on my chest. 'But you're *not?*'

'I got out of it.'

'Wise move.'

I shrugged. 'Lucky for some.'

I glanced over my shoulder, searching for Jay but no longer expecting to find him. Ed used the momentary lull to raise his hands in the air and yell, 'Come on, fellers, let's go toast the health of our winner here!'

That stirred the crowd back up and with a roar they started filing back inside. I stayed where I was, letting them brush past me, and so did Ed. Soon it was only me, him, the farmer, his boy and the two unconscious bully-boys left in the yard, and then even the farmer staggered away with his son helping him go.

Ed glanced down at his two hired men. 'You ain't lost none of your old style,' he remarked.

'That makes two of us, I reckon.'

'Now, I can't help it if my boys sometimes get a mite … over-enthusuastic, can I?'

'You're running crooked games, Ed. Best you clean, 'em up before someone gets hurt permanent.'

'You know, for a man with no authority, you still sound like a lawman to me,' he said. Then he hooked a thumb in the direction of the tent. 'Look, why don't we bury our diff'rences, Jim? Christ, it's been six years, hasn't it? We're older an' wiser now, ain't we? Come on, I'll buy you a drink.'

I shook my head. 'Nuh-huh. I still remember the kind of effects your whiskey can have on a body.'

His response was indifferent. 'Suit yourself.'

As he turned to go back inside I said, right out of the blue, 'By the way, what was Jay Bannon doing around here?'

I watched him closely, saw something flare in his dark, button-bright eyes at mention of the name before he realised it and moved to stifle it. He gave a careless shrug. 'Who's Bannon?'

I tried to bluff. 'I heard he's been running a faro layout for you ever since he got here.'

He shook his head, his expression elaborately dismissive. 'Nah. You must've heard wrong. Only men I got working for me I brought in with me.'

Another of his hired men came out through the tent flp. lugging a wooden bucket slopping with water. He dumped half of it over the first thug I'd laid out, the rest over the second. As soon as the water hit them they lurched upright, choking and gasping and cursing a blue streak. Ed said meaningfully, 'Maybe you better get out of here now, Jim.'

I was inclined to agree. Every muscle in my body

was throbbing to the same beat, and I was still feeling sick with it. I was forty five, and I'd had enough of fighting to last me a lifetime. And while I doubted very much if either Cal or his friend would fancy making any more mischief tonight, I couldn't be certain.

I stooped to pick up my fallen hat and finger-brushed my long hair back off my face before putting it back on. 'I'll see you again, Ed,' I said without intonation.

He made a welcoming gesture with his hands, and said sarcastically, 'Glad to hear it. Maybe we'll have that drink together yet.'

I left him there and stumbled back along the dogtrot. Homesteaders were still lingering at the far end, waiting to get a look at me. But if they were expecting something special, I reckoned they were in for a disappointment.

'Mister?'

I'd reached the mouth of the dogtrot. When I looked around, I saw the beat-up farmer, still leaning on his red-eyed son. He stuck out one hand and offered me a game smile that reopened the splits in his lips and showed me the gaps where he'd lost a couple of teeth. 'Freddie here says I owe you my life.'

'Forget it.'

He shook his head, then winced, 'No,' he replied. 'I'm beholden. I'd offer to give you somethin' for your trouble, but them sumbitches took me for near ever'thin' but what I keep stashed in my socks.'

'Just get back on to your wagon and look to your wounds,' I told him, rougher than I meant to. 'And think twice before you go back into a place like this.'

'Ayuh,' he said. 'I'll sure do that.'

What remained of the crowd was dispersing, and

loneliness was creeping back over me. Again I pictured Jay's face in my mind. I'd been right. He *was* here. But where was he *now*? And how long would he stay, now that he knew I was here as well?

Favouring my side, I set off for my campsite, no longer hungry, just hurting and tired … and aching to meet up with that sonofabitch again.

I left the tent city behind me and limped tiredly back to my camp. Moonlight painted the trees and brush with molten silver, but I was in no mood to appreciate the beauty of it all.

The walk seemed to last for ever. I stopped a couple of times, when my side started to pain me bad, or when I thought I was going to puke. But at length I spied the silhouette of my sorrel, grazing peacefully where I'd left him picketed earlier that day, and when he heard me approaching, his big head came up and he gave a nicker of welcome that made me smile a little.

I went over to him and let him nuzzle my sore left hand while I rubbed the velvety skin between his eyes with my right. I was still thinking about Jay and Ed, wondering if there really *was* a connection between them, and if so, what it was.

Distantly I said, 'Hello, boy –'

– and that's when someone took a shot at me.

A moment of blind confusion followed. As the horse started tugging desperately at his picket-pin, stretching the halter-rope so tight that I thought it might snap, I threw myself flat and rolled away from his stamping hooves. Meanwhile, the slug whined overhead and chopped into some foliage aways off to my left.

I snaked away from the horse, came up behind some brush and drew my Colt. My heart was driving hard and I was telling myself that this was turning into a hell of a busy night.

But after that initial spurt of action, I forced myself to stay absolutely still. I didn't even breathe. My sorrel was still pulling at his picket-pin and making uneasy noises, and I wished he'd shut up so that I could listen for any sounds the other man might be making.

As it was, I couldn't see him and I couldn't hear him. I'd chosen my campsite because it was sheltered by cottonwoods and because the brush gave me some privacy from all the people at Oklahoma Station. But now, in the poor starlight, it meant that my would-be assassin could be hiding anywhere.

Then –

I heard the faint rustle of leaf against leaf about sixty feet off to the west, and tensed. I brought the gun up, ready for use, but that was my only movement. Long seconds ticked by. There were no other sounds. But that didn't mean he was staying where he was. Even now he could be working around behind me.

Without looking down, I felt around with my left hand and fastened my fingers on a fist-sized rock. I picked it up, hefted it, judged it to be heavy enough for my purpose. Drawing in a shallow breath, I lobbed it across the hollow.

It fell into the scrub over there with a snapping of twigs and almost immediately a lance of amber flame exploded from the darkness fifty feet ahead of me, alongside another spiteful, cracking hand gun blast.

I sent two fast shots back at the muzzle-flash, then powered up and ran for some thicker trees behind me, figuring to work *my* way around behind *him*. He fired another shot that buzzed through the darkness. I heard it slam into a tree-trunk twenty feet away, then turned at the waist and fired again. Then I threw myself down, spraying leaves and red dirt everywhere. I rolled, came up behind a spindly cottonwood and then recocked the Colt.

Another shot screamed across the hollow. It didn't even come close, which meant that the bushwhacker, whoever he was, no longer knew where I was.

I listened for a moment more. At first there was nothing to hear apart from the sounds of my frightened horse and some distant bangings and clatterings drifting out from Oklahoma Station.

Then I heard the other man moving again – *away* from me this time – and my lip curled in disgust. Damn him, he'd come here expecting to shoot me from hiding, only I'd been hard to kill and now he wanted to get out of here before I shot *him* instead.

I thought, *Hell with that* –

I came up as well, and started after him. He must have heard me, because next moment another shot crashed out of the shadows. I flung myself flat, awakening fresh pain in my battered body, fired twice back at him and rolled quickly away from the tell-tale gunflashes. He returned fire, wildly now, then continued his retreat.

I pushed myself erect and went after him. If it was Jay out there, I might never get a better chance to settle with him than this. Racing through the spindly timber, I thumbed back the Colt's hammer again. Moonlight fell on a clearing ahead, and I saw a shadowy figure heading for a ground-hitched horse on the far side. I yelled, '*Hold it!*' and though he stumbled momentarily, he kept going.

'*Hold it, damn you!*'

He turned, fired another round from the hip. I went sideways as the bullet slapped a hot wind into my face. Instinctively I tried to return fire, but nothing happened. I swore again, because I realised that my gun was empty.

Dammit, there was no way I could hope to reload before he made good his escape. All I could do was watch him hurl himself up across leather, yank his protesting mount's head around and kick the beast into a mad canter away into the cloaking night.

'*Dammit!*' I yelled, feeling powerless and furious all at once. '*Dammit!*'

I slept real light that night, as you can imagine, and when I woke up next morning I was as stiff as a board. My arms felt like lead weights, my ribs were sore and I had the mother of all headaches, but somehow I managed to get up, build a fire and then hobble down to the nearby stream. I washed and felt better for it, then started struggling back to camp like a ninety year old.

My route took me through the clearing where the bushwhacker had quartered his horse the night before. In the loose soil his tracks were clear to read. But there was something strange about them that made me bend and examine them closer, a string of shallow, regularly-spaced holes that seemed to run along beside them and end when I came to the spot at which the man's horse had waited for him.

I didn't know what to make of them, and to be honest I felt so stiff and uncomfortable that I couldn't seem to get my mind to work properly. With a wince I straightened up out of my crouch and staggered on back to camp.

I fixed myself some bacon and beans and was just stuffing rough-cut into my pipe for an after-breakfast smoke when I heard hoofbeats coming in from the west. Part of a second later my Colt was in my hand, its short blued barrel stabbing ahead to greet the newcomer.

He came around some low scrub aboard a fine-looking blood bay horse and when he saw me sitting on the far side of the small fire with a gun in my hand he reined in, put up his free palm and said in a deep, confident voice, 'Hold your fire, mister. I come peaceable.'

There was something familiar about him that made me frown. He was tall and spare, dressed in a black suit, boiled shirt and string tie, and his crossed gunbelts carried matched Peacemakers. And that wasn't all. The star-and-crescent shield of a Deputy US Marshal winked brightly on his lapel.

'Ned?' I asked in disbelief. 'That you up there, Ned Brooding?'

Moving slowly, he reached up and pushed his broad-brimmed black hat back, and as sunlight fell onto his long, teak-hard face, I saw that it was indeed him.

He squinted across the sixty feet that separated us and leaned slightly forward in his creaking saddle. 'That's never you, is it, Jim?'

I stood up with a grunt and slipped the Colt back into leather, heartened by the unexpected appearance of such an old and valued friend. 'Come on in and see for yourself, Ned. You fetch a mug with you? I got coffee boiling.'

He heeled his horse closer, then swung down, tethered him to some scrub beside my own and hustled over to clasp my hand and pump it with genuine warmth. He said, 'Goddlemighty, Jim, what the hell're *you* doin' up this way? Don't tell me you got tired of herdin' cows?' Before I could answer, he inspected my face with a question clear in his sharp hazel eyes. 'Judas Priest, what happened to you?'

I tried to make light of it. 'Had a run-in with a bull buffalo.'

'I take it you lost?'

'You should see the buffalo,' I replied. 'But what the hell are *you* doing here, Ned? You're the last person I expected to see.'

'Aw, that's easy. They sent me out to try an' keep order among the settlers till the twenty-second.'

'Tough job.'

'You said it. I got deputies, a'course, and the army's a help, but ... well, I daresay you've already seen the size of the problem for yourself. Still, it's only for a couple more days now. Once the Rush's over an' all these settlers're busy puttin' down roots in The District, they can start lookin' after themselves.'

He was of an age with me, part Cherokee, with a sharp, straight nose, a wide, lipless mouth and a single braid of raven-black hair hanging down his back. He was one of the best men Judge Parker had working for him. We'd partnered each other a time or two, and he was a fast, accurate shooter with a mind that thrived on puzzles.

I felt his eyes boring into me now, searching my

face. 'What *are* you doing here, Jim?' he asked. 'Folks tell me there was some shootin' out this way las' night. That's why I come out here this mornin'.'

Sobering, I said, 'I'm looking for a feller name of Bannon.'

He read something in my tone and said, 'What is it, law business?'

'Personal.'

'What'd he do?'

'He killed Clare.'

He took the news hard because he'd known Clare for most of her life, and no matter how many times it happens, you never think you're going to outlive someone who's so much younger than you are. Beneath his coppery skin he paled noticeably and he didn't speak for a minute or so. Finally he swallowed and said, 'I'll have that coffee now,' and hurried back over to his horse and fished a tin mug out of his nearside saddlebag.

'What happened?' he asked as I filled the mug a moment later.

I told him and at the end of it I described Jay and asked Ned if he'd run into him in the last week or so.

He shook his head. 'Not that I recall. But if I do …'

'He's mine,' I said quietly.

He eyed me steadily, then nodded.

'So that's what all the shootin' was about las' night?' he asked. 'Bannon?'

'Maybe.'

'What does that mean?'

'I'm not sure yet.' I fired up my pipe at last. The tobacco had a soothing effect on me. 'You know Ed Vallance's set up business here?'

'Hell, half the scum in the Territory's set up business here. These settlers, they're easy pickin's. I spend most of my time jus' tryin' to protect 'em from themselves. But you've lost me. How does Ed figure in this?'

I told him about seeing Jay at Ed's place the previous night, and Ed's obvious recognition of his name when I'd thrown it at him.

'You sayin' Bannon's workin' for Ed?' Ned mused, rubbing his chin. 'It's possible, I guess. Ed allus did surround himself with a pretty tough crew.'

He finished his coffee and flipped away the grounds, then straightened back up. 'Well, watch yourself, Jim. An' go easy. You start mixin' it up with Ed Vallance an' things're apt to turn mean.'

I looked at him sidelong. 'You're not trying to warn me off, are you, Ned?'

'All I'm doin' is askin' you to spare a thought for Nan. She's a right fine woman, Jim. But she's already lost a daughter. Las' thing she needs now is to lose her husband as well.'

I nodded and we shook hands again.

'I'll keep my eyes and ears open,' he promised. 'If Bannon's still in Oklahoma Station, we'll find him.'

I put my eyes on the distant confusion of tents and wagons, and wished I could share his optimism.

SIX

I watched Ned mount up and ride away, and once he was gone, the hollow was an emptier, bleaker place.

I finished my smoke, then knocked the dottle out of my pipe, blew through it, knocked it into my palm twice more and then slipped it into my shirt pocket.

Last night's fight had left me feeling stove-up and brittle. But I couldn't afford the luxury of a slow recovery. With the Land Rush now only two days away, time was running out for me. I had to make every second count.

With effort I saddled up and walked the sorrel into the temporary town. Towards the centre, enterprising vendors were selling buckets of water for a dollar each. I found a makeshift barbershop nearby and paid over the odds for a tub of hot water. About an hour later I climbed out of the tub, dried myself off and climbed back into my clothes. As I'd hoped, the hot water had loosened up some of the cramps and I found I was able to get around more easily. Better still, it had cleared my head so that I was able to think more sharply.

Outside again, I swung back into the saddle. It was late morning, and to every point of the compass the tent city was all bustle and rush. Men were gathering in clusters to discuss crops, the weather, the impending Rush: women were gossiping, marketing or rubbing shirts and dresses against soapy washboards; and children were stumbling or trotting around and trying to catch flies. Anticipation and expectancy were thick in the warm air.

During my soak I'd had plenty of time to think. But it was Ed Vallance, not Jay, who had dominated my thoughts. He knew more than he was letting on, I felt certain. There was some link between him and Jay, I could sense it.

That made Ed the best chance I had of finding my daughter's killer. Which, in turn, meant that whether I cared to or not, I had to go back to his canvas saloon and force some answers out of him.

I heeled the sorrel into motion, skirted around all the confusion and headed deeper into the centre of the sprawling town. When I reached my destination, I tied up at a rope corral nearby and went inside.

The saloon was immersed in a dull green twilight, and I had to wait a moment for my eyes to adjust to it. A few down-at-heel homesteaders were nursing drinks up at the plank-and-barrel bar, a few more were seated at the scattered, scratched tables that had been set up on the loose-plank, sawdusted floor. I paused just inside the entrance and looked for Ed or either of the men I'd fought the night before, but they were nowhere in sight.

After a couple more seconds I went up to the least-crowded end of the bar, intending to ask the burly barkeep where Ed was hiding himself, when a low, easy voice to my left said, 'Looking for someone, Allison?'

I glanced down at the man who was sitting at a table close by, his chair wedged into the space where two sides of the big, patched tent met to form a corner. He looked angular and darkly handsome, thirtyish, with cropped black hair brushed back off his high forehead and a face that was dominated by two cool green eyes and a set of high, very prominent cheekbones. He wore an old cavalry shirt tucked into dark blue pants, and a brown paper cigarette projected from between the first and second fingers of his right hand, spiralling grey smoke straight up into the air. He held a schooner of beer in his left hand, and a big, converted Navy Colt lay on the table beneath his right.

My eyes followed the slow, apparently aimless fingertip caresses he lavished on the weapon. You touched a woman that way, not a gun. Then I put my gaze back onto his face and nodded. 'Looking for Ed,' I replied.

'Ed's not here. Will I do?'

'That depends. Who're you?'

'Ringer,' he said. 'Missouri John Ringer. I kind of run things when Ed's not around. You know … take care of any little problems that crop up.' He raised the schooner in his left hand. 'Buy you a drink?'

I walked over to his table. 'No thanks. Where's Ed?'

He put the cigarette to his mouth, drew on it, then went back to fiddling with the gun. 'Oh, around.'

'With Bannon?' I hedged.

He smiled. 'Who's Bannon?'

'You know, that's just what Ed said.'

'Well, who *is* he?' Another drag on the cigarette. 'Or who do you *think* he is?'

I turned the question around on him. 'Who do *you* think he is, Ringer?'

He made a careless gesture with his shoulders. 'You've been asking for him right the way through Oklahoma Station. You say he killed your daughter.'

'There's no "say" about it. He *did* kill her.'

'Well, be that as it may, you won't find him here.'

'He was here last night.'

'So were a lot of other people. We call 'em customers.'

'And Ed knows all his customers by name, is that what you're telling me?'

'Some.'

His fingertips slid over the cold, dark iron of the Colt on the table in front of him. He traced a few more squiggles across the grips, then put the cigarette back into his mouth. 'It's like they say. Word gets around.'

'Maybe I'd better come back later,' I said. 'Speak to Ed about it.'

He shook his head. 'No.'

I'd turned halfway away from him. Now I checked the movement and faced him again. 'Say what?'

'Don't come back, Allison. Not today, not ever. Ed's a busy man. He doesn't need the extra hassle. Now, you've asked after Bannon, and I've told you he's just a customer, maybe not even that. Take my advice. *Stay* told. You'll live longer that way.'

He went back to fondling the gun again, then raised the schooner to his lips and took a slow drink. I heard the pads of his fingers rubbing against the gun, the gun itself making little rasping metal sounds against the scratched wood of the table.

I said, 'Let's get something straight, Ringer. I've got no argument with you, not if you really *don't* know who Bannon is or where I can find him. But I've got the damnedest notion that you know him, all right – *and* where I can find him, too.' I put my knuckles on the table so that I could lean over him. 'I think you're *shielding* him, Ringer, you and Ed. I don't know why yet, but I'd put money on it.'

His left cheek twitched like he'd been slapped, and suddenly his eyelids came down so that he looked like a drowsy, dangerous snake. 'You know something, Allison? You got a big mouth. It's gonna be the death of you someday.'

'All I want to know is where I can find Bannon.'

'And I told you, old-timer – I don't *know* any Bannon. A'course, if you're calling me a liar …'

I sucked in a deep breath and said quietly, 'Why are you so dead set on fighting me, Ringer?'

He said, 'Man calls me a liar –'

'That's got nothing to do with it,' I said over him. 'One way or another you've been trying awful hard to pick a fight with me ever since I came in here. Now why *is* that? Ed put you up to it? Bannon?'

His lips curled. '"Bannon, Bannon, Bannon",' he mimicked.

'Well, which of 'em is it? Or is it both of 'em together?'

'You're pushing real hard now, Allison,' he warned.

'Maybe that's because I haven't heard any straight answers yet.'

'So you *are* calling me a liar,' he hissed. His cool green eyes fixed on mine and stayed there even when he moved the rest of his face in a slow headshake. 'Ah, Allison,' he murmured in quiet disapproval. 'You shouldn't've done that.'

I pushed up off the table. My eyes flickered down to the gun beneath his fingers. He was still stroking and fondling the weapon, but his movements were coming faster now, shakier, more urgent.

I knew he was going to make a play for the gun.

But I hadn't come here for that. All at once the situation was turning dangerous, and keeping my hands well out from my sides, I backed slowly away from him. I didn't want to shoot him and neither did I want to get shot. But he seemed determined to railroad me into confrontation.

I felt the eyes of the men up at the bar shuttling between him and me. There was some shuffling as they edged further down to the other end of the makeshift bar, out of range.

Ringer kept toying with his gun. I said, 'Don't even *think* about it, Ringer.'

'It's too late for that,' he replied in a low voice. 'Man insults me, he pays the price.'

He sounded mad. *Sounded* it. But I knew he wasn't any such thing. That was just an act, put on for the benefit of the men watching us. He'd deliberately orchestrated this confrontation for reasons I didn't understand, and he was making it sound like *I* was the one set on causing trouble, so that afterwards, once I lay dead at his feet, it would look as if he'd only acted in self-defence.

I knew there would be no reasoning with him, not now. So I did the last thing he expected me to do. I turned away from him, just like he wasn't there, and said to the barkeep, 'Tell Ed I'll be in to have a word with him later,' and then I started to leave, steady, straight in the back, shoulders squared, unhurried, trying to give no sign of just how coiled tight I was inside.

Ringer's voice whipped out behind me.

'Allison! Come back here!'

I kept going.

'What *are* you?' he cried. 'A damn' coward?'

That was strong talk. But he could think what he liked. They all could. The truth was that I couldn't afford trouble. It might mean delay. And delay was something I certainly didn't need right then.

'Turn around and fight!' yelled Ringer.

I got as far as the tent flap, and then I heard the legs of his chair scraping back across the loose-plank floor and I knew he'd got to his feet.

'*Allison!*'

Something else had entered his tone now, and all at once I knew that this wasn't going to work, that I wasn't just going to be allowed to walk out of here scot-free after all.

I pulled to a stop to one side of the exit so that I wouldn't make any better target of myself than I could help, and slowly turned to face him.

I was right. He'd gotten up, shoved his Colt into its holster and come around the table to fight me.

Then I noticed something else besides.

He was leaning on an old, well-worn cane, the fingers of his left hand folded strangle-tight around the curved handle. His left leg was badly twisted, as if maybe he'd broken it many years before and never had it set right.

I hadn't been expecting that, and it showed on

my face.

Now he limped another couple of steps towards me, and the cane went *bump, bump, bump, bump* against the boards right alongside him. He was smiling at my surprise. 'Ayuh,' he said with a nod. 'I bet that makes you feel *really* big, doesn't it? Pickng a fight with a *cripple?*'

I shook my head slowly. 'I'm not the one picking the fight,' I replied. But I don't know why I bothered to say that. I knew he was only drawing attention to his disability for the benefit of the onlookers, to get them even further on his side, and perhaps to put me off my guard.

He said, 'Well, Allison. I'm waiting.' And the fingers of his right hand flexed above the Colt's walnut butt.

I looked at him some more, into his face, his eyes, down to the flexing fingers of his gunhand, and then across to the whitened knuckles fixed around the cane.

The cane ...

The cane ...

I felt knots tighten in my brow as I looked at it. I thought about the tracks the bushwhacker had left behind him the night before. Those shallow, round imprints that ran alongside the bootprints ...

Suddenly I knew what had made them and who the bushwhacker had been.

My eyes came back up to Ringer's face and this time whatever he saw in them unnerved him. I said softly, 'Why is it, Ringer? Why does Ed want me out of the way so bad that he sent you to cut me down last night?'

His fingers flexed faster. 'I don't know what the hell you're talking about,' he bluffed. But he did. It was written all over him.

I took a pace back towards him, feeling the anger building inside me. I knew that Ed wouldn't risk making trouble with me for what had happened six years earlier. That was water over the dam. And it might jeopardise whatever scams he was working here now. So it had to be something else, something more immediate. But what? Jay?

Hell, it always came back to Jay.

'No need to deny it, Ringer,' I said. 'I know it was you out there taking pot-shots at me last night. What I want to know now is *why?*'

He curled his lip at me again. 'First you call me a liar. Now you're calling me a backshooter. Christ Almighty, you really *do* want a fight, don't you?'

All at once I saw him go stiff and I said, 'Ringer –'

But it was too late – he was already going for his gun, and to hell with whatever was wrong with his leg, he was damn' sudden, just about the fastest gun-thrower I think I'd ever seen.

His Colt was out and in his hand, blurring up and spitting flame even as my own fingers were closing on my Army .476, and I was still drawing when the roar of his pistol filled the big tent.

But like the man said; being fastest isn't always enough. Instinctively I'd taken a step aside, which was just as well because his bullet ripped through the canvas flap where I'd just been standing.

I brought my own Colt up and thumbed back the hammer, but Ringer was already correcting his aim, and the muzzle of his gun was flashing around to beckon me like a one-way passage to eternity.

He fired again and missed again, because I'd dropped to one knee by then, and I heard his second bullet slap through the canvas behind me.

Inside the saloon, pandemonium reigned as barkeep and customers alike stampeded for cover. Cursing, Ringer thumbed back his Colt-hammer for another shot, but now it was my turn. Teeth clenched, I fired right at him and saw dust puff up off his old blue shirt where my bullet hit him in the chest.

He staggered under the impact of the bullet and discharged his own gun into the plank floor. The cane left his grip and clattered at his feet. I straightened up, knowing that I'd killed him but just waiting for him to actually die. He looked awful, that's the only word I can think to describe him. The blood had drained from his face to leave him the colour of dirty soap, and he was stumbling around like a man with ice underfoot, trying to reach for the edge of the bar.

He made it, steadied himself, looked down at the dark blood raining out across his shirtfront, and then he turned his cool green eyes back to me and he snarled something and brought his gun up again.

We both yelled together.

'No more, Ringer!'/ 'Damn you!'

I shot him again. He coughed and hunched up under the force of the second bullet, so that he was hugging himself when he crashed down onto his knees, and from there smashed face-first against the loose boards.

I stood like a statue for a couple of moments, until I was sure there wasn't going to be any more trouble. Then I went over to the body and toed it onto its back.

Missouri John Ringer glared up at me, as dead as yesterday.

I felt eyes on me and looked up. The other patrons were staring at me like I was some kind of monster. I flicked my eyes to the barkeep. His hands were out of sight under the bar. I said one word. 'Reach.'

He brought his hands up, empty.

It was absolutely quiet in there now, apart from all the excited sounds drifting in from outside. I fixed the barkeep with a stern eye and asked him where Ed was. He said he didn't know. I asked him again and he shook his head and said honest, he didn't know, Ed didn't tell him things like that.

Well, that was probably true. But when I kept staring at him he let his eyes drop away from mine and finally allowed as how he'd heard Ed say something about having some business to attend to south of here, on the edge of the temporary town.

'All right,' I said, satisfied. 'I'm leaving now, and I don't want any more trouble. But you try reaching under that bar again before I'm gone and I'll be leaving *two* bodies behind me. You understand what I'm saying?'

He nodded and stayed exactly as he was, hands up and frightened-looking. I backed out of there, shoved roughly through the growing crowd outside and got my horse.

I rode south, determined to find Ed and get some answers. But I rode in a kind of fog, because the speed with which all of this had happened had left me dazed, and suddenly I felt that the situation was getting out of my grasp.

I rode the whole of the southernmost perimeter without finding him. I asked a few of the homesteaders there if they'd seen him around, but they hadn't. I rode back the other way, searching, always searching, but there was still no sign of him. The afternoon grew hot and my joints started to seize up again, and that was just what I needed to cap it all off.

At length I reined in and leaned forward with my arms folded across my pommel, sweating hard and frustrated as hell. If Ed really *had* come south, I hadn't been able to find him.

Dammit.

Finally I headed back to his saloon. There was nowhere else to go. But when I got within twenty yards of the place, I saw a couple of horses standing ground-hitched out front that I didn't like the look of. Don't ask me what it was, just another one of those lawman's hunches of mine, I guess. They were the sleek, muscular horses of men who did a lot of riding, and the well-used long guns I saw jutting from scabbards buckled under right-side fenders hinted at quite a bit of fighting, as well.

I figured they were the horses of a couple of Ned Brooding's deputies.

I reined in again and thought about that. The deputies had likely come out to investigate the shooting. Which meant that sooner or later they'd want a word with me.

Well, that was too bad. It was just going to have to be later, because I couldn't spare the time right then.

I turned the sorrel away and rode east, back to camp. With no other course of action open to me, I decided to wait an hour or so and then ride back in and brace Ed when the law was no longer around. With any luck, my joints might have loosened up again by then.

I put the town behind me and thought some more about Ringer. The afternoon was well-advanced and already the lowering orange sun was unrolling long shadows on the ground in front of me. It didn't bother me that I'd had to kill Ringer. He'd had that coming. No – it was the *why* of it all that kept nagging at me, and I knew I'd get no rest until I found an answer.

I rode on for another quarter of a mile, still trying to puzzle it all out, then turned a bend in the rough, overgrown trail and smelled coffee on the air.

It was then that I reined in fast and drew my gun.

A man with his back to me had made himself at home in my camp sixty feet ahead. He'd kindled a fire and fixed himself a pot of java and was even now hunkering beside the stone ring and pouring himself a refill, completely unaware of my presence.

Raising my voice I said, 'Hold it.'

But he didn't. He leapt up, dropping the coffee pot into the fire and slopping coffee from his – my – mug, and stumbled around to face me, looking guilty as hell.

As the coffee pot emptied into the fire the flames sizzled and spat, and grey smoke began to cloud up between us like a lace curtain. I looked at him. He was short and thin, somewhere in his early forties, dressed in homespun pants, a sack coat, no shirt, just a faded red undervest, and a floppy-brimmed dark hat. The man himself was tanned, as punched-about as I was, with very pale blue eyes and a heavy jaw sandpapered by fine blond stubble.

'Ah … Mr Allison?' he said, raising his big hands in a gesture of surrender. 'D-don't shoot, Mr Allison, it's only me, Tully McFarland.'

My brows met in a frown. McFarland? Who the hell was McFarland?

'Uh … hope you didn't mind me cookin' up some coffee,' he went on, wearing a sickly smile now. ''S just … well, they told me you'd set up camp out here, only when I got here you was nowhere around, an' I didn't know how long it'd be afore you got back, so … uh …'

I gave up trying to place him, I just came right out with it. 'Do I know you, mister?'

He looked surprised by that. '*McFarland,*' he said again. 'You stopped them damn' pugs killin' me last night.'

At last recognition came. He was the farmer with the split lips and gappy teeth. I slid the Colt back into leather and walked the sorrel in closer as McFarland turned and bent to retrieve the blackening coffee pot.

'What are you doing out this way, McFarland?' I asked, dismounting, loosening the horse's girth and leading him over to some brush, where I turned his reins once around a leafy offshoot.

He said, 'Well, Mr Allison … it's about last night.'

'I thought I told you to forget about that.'

'Ayuh, yessir, you did. But … but I told you I was beholden.'

I went over to him. He was shifting his weight from one leg to the other, still anxious and uncomfortable. I guessed I'd given him a bad scare, pointing my gun at him the way I had. It's a sobering thing, staring down a gun-muzzle, knowing you're *that* close to stopping a bullet. You never get used to it, and any man who tells you otherwise is a damn' liar.

I took the pot from him and set it down. 'Well,

I'm telling you again, McFarland. Forget it.'

'But … I come to try an' repay you, Mr Allison.'

'I don't want your money.'

He gave a short, ironic snort. 'I got no money for you,' he said. 'Though you'd be welcome to it if I had. I got some *information*.'

'Information?'

He bobbed his head and the loose brim of his old dark hat flopped around his face like the ears of a mule. 'They say you been askin' all over for the man that murdered your daughter,' he said. 'Feller called Bannon?'

Something fluttered in my stomach as I looked at him there in the clean yellow-orange light of the late afternoon, with flies darting and buzzing all around us. 'What about it?' I said cautiously.

'I know where you can find him, Mr Allison,' McFarland replied. 'That's what I come to tell you. I know where you can find this feller Bannon.'

I lurched forward and grabbed him by the arms, and when I spoke again my voice was a snap and a growl. 'Where is he?'

He winced under the pressure of my grip, because he was probably just as stiff and sore as I was, and remembering myself, I let go of him and gestured an apology.

He said, 'Early this mornin' he come prowlin' around the section where I been keepin' my wagon. He didn't come right out an' say it, but it was obvious, he was there lookin' for sooners. Heard later that he reckons he knows a route into The District that the army hasn't got covered, an' says he'll lead as many as wants to go to a prime spot along Rattler Creek for twenty dollars a head.'

I let my breath go in a long hiss and shook my head slowly. There was that word again, *sooners*. I might have known that Jay would be mixed up in something like that, offering to smuggle anyone with enough money to pay into the unassigned lands so that they could stake their claims ahead of time.

'Did he get any takers?' I asked.

'Well, they weren't lettin' on, but I could tell. They's about a dozen of 'em.'

'Where is he now, then? Bannon?'

'That I *don't* know. But he's meetin' 'em tonight, seven o'clock, at a place called Lane Ridge.' He saw the question in my look and added, 'It's about fifteen miles west of here. That's where you'll catch him, Mr Allison.'

It was the most promising lead I'd had so far, and it chased away all the aches and frustrations and put new life into me. Nodding to McFarland I said, 'Thanks,' but in truth there were no words to properly express my gratitude to him.

I turned away and went over to my horse. By my estimate, it was four o'clock or thereabouts. That gave me three hours to locate Lane Ridge and then find myself a good vantagepoint from which to await Jay's arrival.

But even as I started to retighten the sorrel's clinchstrap, I heard a gun click to full-cock behind me, and I stiffened as a rough voice barked, 'All right, Allison, that's far enough! Put your hands up and step away from that horse. You're under *arrest!*'

SEVEN

Of all the things you don't or can't argue with in this life, a cocked sixgun is right at the top of the list. That's why I did like I was told without complaint, just put my hands up, backed away from the horse, then turned around real slow so that I could get a look at the man who'd apprehended me.

In fact there were two of them, fifty feet away on the other side of the hollow, and they were sitting astride the horses I'd spotted earlier, outside Ed's saloon. Beneath their big hats they had a hard look, the pair of them. The first was about twenty eight or thirty, the second a couple of years younger. The first was broad across the belly, with a full brown beard and cold little blue eyes. The second was shorter, leaner and darker, maybe of Italian extraction. They wore Levis and plain cotton shirts, and star-and-crescent shields on the lapels of their dusty box jackets.

Both of them had their sidearms out and pointed my way.

Ed Vallance was perched on a heavy black horse with a white blaze on its forehead a few yards behind them. Caution and uncertainty were pinching his fleshy face tight because he didn't know how I was going to take to being arrested.

Without turning his head, the first deputy said to his partner, 'Take his gun and cuff him, Frankie.' Then, while Frankie dismounted and came over to do just that, he said to me, 'You're under arrest for the murder of John Henry Ringer, Allison. You got anything you want to say about that?'

'Only that it was self-defence, not murder,' I replied.

'Well, that's not what Mr Vallance here says –'

'I don't give a damn what Mr Vallance says,' I cut in. 'Just ask the men who saw it happen.'

'We've already asked 'em,' said Frankie, taking my gun and shoving it into his waistband. 'They say you went into Mr Vallance's place spoiling for a fight. When Ringer asked you to leave, there was an argument. You went for your gun. Ringer tried to defend himself. You shot him.'

I looked at him as he reached up and pulled my arms down and around to the small of my back so that he could fasten his heavy iron manacles around my wrists.

'It sounds to me like you've been asking the wrong men,' I grated, beginning to see how this business was shaping up and not liking it one bit. 'It was Ringer picked the fight. He went for his gun first. He fired two shots that missed. I fired two shots that didn't.'

The first deputy looked at me with the flat, seen-it-all before expression that all lawmen get sooner or later. 'Tell it to the judge,' he muttered. Then he hipped around to address Ed. 'You'll be required to give evidence, of course, Mr Vallance.'

Ed assumed a look of piety, the Janus-faced sonofabitch. 'I'll be there, Deputy Baker,' he replied. 'John Ringer was a good man, and I liked him a lot. I want to make sure his killer hangs high.'

Now that I was cuffed, some of his old swagger was coming back, and he glared straight at me as he said it. When the first deputy, Baker, turned away from him, I saw a faint, triumphant smile tease the edges of Ed's thick-lipped mouth, and that just about confirmed the worst.

I swore under my breath. I'd been afraid that Ringer's shooting would end up like this, that Ed would twist the facts all out of shape and import some 'witnesses' of his own to confirm them. His plan was more subtle than Ringer's had been, but both men had been working towards the same end – to get me out of the way.

'Mr Allison?'

It was McFarland, watching everything through confused, scared eyes.

'Is … is it true? You killed an innocent man?'

I looked at him and shook my head.

'All right,' said Deputy Baker, turning businesslike now. 'Get him up on his horse, Frankie, and then get all his gear together. He won't be coming back here in a hurry.'

I wanted to fight them, to delay what was inevitable, but I knew it was futile. My helplessness, especially when I'd been so close to catching up with Jay, made me feel sick. 'You're making a big mistake here, Baker,' I said.

He arched an eyebrow. 'What, in enforcing the law?'

Frankie shoved me back towards my horse. He tightened the girth down and when I put my foot in the stirrup he boosted me up into the saddle.

After that we got our horses moving at a walk

back to Oklahoma Station, and I can tell you now that I've never felt so powerless and downright degraded before in my life.

'Baker?' I called about ten minutes later.

Baker, riding at the head of our small column, tilted his head back at me.

'I want to see Ned Brooding when we reach the Station,' I said. 'He'll straighten this out.'

Baker said, 'You can't. Brooding rode out on business this morning.'

That was bad news. 'Well, when will he be back?'

'Tonight. Maybe.'

My teeth clamped together and I swore again. Tonight. Dammit, tonight was going to be too late.

When we reached the outskirts of the tent town, Ed said his farewells to the two deputies, threw me one last, loaded glance and then peeled away, heading for his saloon. Watching him go, I wondered if, on top of everything else, he'd bribed the deputies to arrest me. It was possible.

I cursed him some more.

Baker and Frankie took me right through the jumbled town to the washed-out grey buildings of Oklahoma Station itself. Frankie helped me dismount, then shoved me up the ramp at the end of the platform and along to the station agent's office, which had been taken over by both the US Marshals and the army.

The room was cluttered and chaotic. Desks, chairs, even camp-beds and bedrolls, were everywhere. I stopped just inside the doorway as every hostile face turned toward me. Then Baker or Frankie pushed me in the back to keep me going forward, and when we went through another door I found myself confronted by a darkened supply

room at the back of the building, into which I was
then unceremoniously thrown.

I caught my balance and turned around. Baker
was already preparing to slam the door on me, but
I stopped him.

'Hey now!' I yelled. 'You not even going to take
these irons off me?'

Baker said, 'No.'

My shoulders dropped. 'Well, at least remember
what I said. I've got to see Brooding the minute he
gets in.'

He grinned. 'You know, I don't see as how you're
in any position to make demands – cripple-killer.'

He slammed the door on me and I listened to the
key turning in the lock. I remember being amazed
at how one man in the middle of fifty thousand can
feel so lonely.

I looked around the makeshift cell. It was gloomy
and unclean. Crates were stacked everywhere, and
other formless junk had been piled wherever there
was a spare space.

I sat down on a crate and wished I could stretch
my arms and relieve some of the cramps in my
shoulders. No matter how I tried, I couldn't shake
the irony of my situation. I knew exactly where I
would find the man I was after at seven o'clock –
now no more than a couple of hours away – and yet
here I was, locked up for a murder that had never
been anything of the kind.

The knowledge tasted like blood on my tongue.

A small window was set high in the facing wall. I
looked up at the brassy sky beyond it, thinking
about the time. Every so often I heard the men in

the outer office coming or going, talking and laughing. Every time I heard a horse outside I wondered if it was Ned, returning from whatever had taken him away, but it wasn't.

Time passed, and the sky darkened. I knew that I had lost the chance to go after Jay, and I thought, *I'm sorry, Clare.*

There were comings and goings, more second-hand circuits of every watch- and clock-face in Oklahoma Station. I felt restless, but knew it would do no good to lose my temper. Instead I shifted around to try and get more comfortable, and flexed my fingers to stop my trapped arms from stiffening up too much. My thoughts turned to home. To Nan. My grandson. The men. Connie Crane. All at once I realised just how long a trail it had been, and I felt tired. Lord, I felt so tired …

I closed my eyes for a moment. At least that's all it seemed to me. But when I heard a key turning in the lock and my eyes snapped open again, the sky beyond the little high window was purple and starry, and I just couldn't think where the time had gone to.

The door swung open and a man came in holding a lantern high. After so long in the dark it hurt my eyes, and I had to look at him through my lashes.

He set the lantern down on a high stack and said, 'Lord above, Jim, what's been happenin' here?'

It was Ned Brooding.

Grown used to silence, my voice was a croak. 'What time is it, Ned?'

He came over, fished a key out of his vest pocket and turned me around so that he could unlock the cuffs. 'Oh, 'bout nine, just after. They tell me you murdered a man, Jim.'

Nine o'clock. Time had well and truly beaten me. Still, it was a relief to be able to move my arms again, and I got up and windmilled them a couple of times to get the circulation going.

Ned was looking at me, the coppery planes of his long face etched in shades of amber and grey by the lantern-glow. 'Jim?'

'I *killed* a man,' I amended at last. 'Murder had nothing to do with it.'

I told him what had happened and when I was through he said, 'I guessed it was somethin' like that.'

'Does that mean I can go now?'

He shook his head. 'You *know* it doesn't.'

'But –'

He put a hand on my shoulder and forced me to sit down again. 'Jim, maybe you better get somethin' straight in that thick skull of yours. You've been charged with *murder*. Now, I've had a look at the papers, an' near as I can see, what it comes down to is Ed Vallance's word against yours. His witnesses against whatever witnesses you can scare up. His *reputation* against yours.' He allowed himself a grim smile. 'From where I'm sittin', I'd say it was no contest. But it's for the courts to decide whether or not you go free, once they've heard all the evidence – such as it is. Not me.'

I finger-brushed my hair back off my forehead. 'I've got to get out of here, Ned. I'm *that* close to nailing Bannon.'

'I'm sorry, Jim. It's out of my hands.'

'Aw, for *crissakes,* Ned!'

But I stopped myself from saying any more, knowing that it would be wrong to take it out on Ned. He was only there to uphold the law, not make it. A moment passed. An idea began to take shape in my head. I thumb-scratched the tuft of hair beneath my bottom lip and hissed, 'Dammit. I was *that* close.'

'What did you turn up?' asked Ned.

I looked at him. 'Something *you* might be interested in.'

'Such as?'

I held back a moment before telling him. 'Jay's smuggling a bunch of sooners into The District tonight. Right about now, in fact.'

'How many?'

'A dozen families that I know about. But if I know Jay, he's been drumming up business right, left and centre, so there's bound to be more. Maybe upwards of fifty wagons.'

That made him straighten up. 'Where's he takin' 'em?' he asked urgently.

I smiled. 'Wouldn't you like to know.'

'Jim ...'

'Aw, come on, Ned, let's not beat around the bush. You do *me* a favour, I'll do *you* a favour.'

'Dammit, you're in no position to −'

'That's what everyone keeps telling me.'

He looked at me for a moment longer, then finally let the air out through his nose. He glanced over his shoulder, just to make sure we were alone. We were. But just to be on the safe side, he went over and pulled the door shut. 'I'm listenin',' he said softly.

'Get me out of here, let me go after him,' I said, speaking fast now. 'I'll tell you where he's headed, but you've got to promise me a couple hours head start. Then, once I've settled with Jay, I'll turn myself back in and let the courts decide whether or not I did what Ed Vallance is claiming.'

He snorted. 'You've got a damn' nerve,' he muttered.

'I'm a desperate man, Ned,' I replied frankly.

He thought about it, I'll give him credit for that, but at the end of it he shook his head just like I knew he would and said, 'I'm sorry, Jim, I can't. They'd have my badge for it, afterwards. I'd be crucified.'

'Why? For setting one man free – temporarily – so's you can send the army out to arrest fifty? They're going to crucify you for that?' I snorted. 'Judas, Ned, you've got the power to turn me loose on my own recognizance, haven't you?'

Iron came into his voice. 'Don't push it, Jim. We been friends a long time. I'd like to keep it that way.'

I sat back. 'All right. If you want Bannon and those fifty sooner families to get away with it …'

'*What* fifty sooner families? You said yourself there's only a dozen you know about for sure.' He walked around the room, exasperated, but when he spoke again he moderated his tone. 'Jim … you know that your pain is my pain. I shouldn't need to tell you that. But I can only stick my neck out so far.'

I nodded in defeat. 'I know.'

'I mean, look at it from my point of view. I can't just set you free so's you can go an' kill another man,' he went on.

'It's all right, Ned. I understand.'

'*But*,' he continued, 'if you give me your word that you'll do everything you can to bring Bannon in alive, I'll make sure he stands trial for Clare's murder.'

I gave him a dark look.

'It's the best I can do, Jim. We'll make him pay. But we'll do it *legally*.'

I didn't care much for that. I wanted Jay to pay for his crimes at *my* hands. But like I said, I was desperate. 'What if I can't bring him in alive?' I asked.

He shrugged. 'If he gives you no option, you'll have to wound him or kill him. I know that. But if you give me your word that you'll at least *try*, well … that'll be good enough for me.'

I stood up, anxious to get moving again. 'All right, Ned,' I told him. 'You've got my word.'

Some of the tightness left his expression. 'Where's he takin' 'em?' he asked again.

I said, 'Rattler Creek.'

He went outside and told one of his men to have my horse saddled. I can just imagine the look his deputy must have given him when he heard that. When he came back to the supply room, he held my Colt in one hand and a cup of lukewarm coffee in the other.

'It's about twenty after nine now,' he said as he handed them both over. 'I'll call out the army at eleven-thirty, or just after.'

I nodded and downed the coffee in one. 'Thanks, Ned. I 'preciate your help.'

'They're gonna bust me for this,' he said mournfully.

'Well, there's always a place for you out at J-Star.'

A brief smile stirred his mouth. 'You know, one of these days I might just take you up on that. I might *have* to.'

He escorted me outside and through the station

agent's commandeered office. I saw Deputy Baker sitting at a desk on the other side of the room and threw him a curt nod. Under the night sky we walked down to the end of the platform and I climbed into the saddle of my waiting horse. I noticed that a long gun had been buckled onto the saddle. I reached down, slid the weapon from its scabbard and examined it briefly. It was a long, heavy, Purdey-made Express shotgun, Ned's own weapon. When I looked down at him he said, 'You never know. It might come in handy.'

'It'll sure do that.'

'I put some extra shells in your saddlebag. Just in case.'

I nodded and slid the Express back home. Extra shells. If I knew Ned, they would be .600-calibre Nitro-Express loads, the most powerful loads then available.

'Thanks.'

'Remember what I told you about Rattler Creek,' he said. 'Ride due north for about two dozen miles an' you'll come to a string of low hills an' scrub oak. You turn west there. About ten, twelve miles beyond that you'll come to the creek. After that, it's just a case of followin' the water till you find the sooners.'

I reached down and clasped his hand. 'I'll be back, Ned.'

I saw his teeth sparkle in the darkness. 'You better be. It's my ass that's on the line, remember.'

I turned the sorrel away from him and we clattered across the railroad tracks and into the unassigned lands. Beneath the pale moonlight, The District was a limitless expanse of low-grassed flats, the occasional cluster of dogwood and pecan, and squat hills, seemingly devoid of human life but no doubt teeming with raccoons, squirrels and prairie dogs ... and cavalry patrols.

I heeled the horse to speed and we galloped away.

Ned had told me that if Jay was leading the sooners to Rattler Creek from Lane Ridge – their prearranged meeting place – he would have to follow a winding, time-consuming course to reach his destination. With luck, my more direct route would allow me to arrive at roughly the same time, depending on how far along Rattler Creek Jay planned to go.

I held the sorrel to a canter until we were no longer in sight of Oklahoma Station, then slowed to a more cautious pace. After all, I was an interloper here as well. I had no more right to be in The District ahead of time than Jay or his sooners, and there was just as much risk of me being spotted and caught by any wandering patrol as there was for him.

So I rode wary and cursed the sounds my horse made in the otherwise still, silent darkness.

The District was vast and apparently empty. Mile after mile wore on with nothing to make me change my mind. It was hard to believe that just thirty six hours from now someone somewhere would fire a gun and homesteaders would swarm across these two million acres like so many greedy ants. For now it was a place of little sound and even less movement, a region that was temporarily out of bounds to the rest of the world.

The sorrel cantered on. The night was warm and cloudy. I slowed once, took out my pocket watch, tilted it to the poor light and read the time.

Ten-thirty already. Another hour and then Ned would be alerting the army.

Twenty minutes later low hills and patchy timber loomed up ahead of me, Ned's first landmark, and I tugged the reins and got the horse turned to the west.

Now the land turned more choppy, all hill and vale, alternately timber, then grass, then a narrow stream, then back to grass, timber and finally more low hills.

It's hard to keep track of time and distance after dark. Night has a way of playing with both. That's why I came upon Rattler Creek almost before I realised it. Swiftly I reined in along the eastern bank, surprised and on my guard. In the moonglow the creek was just a silver ribbon, its edges shaggy with bluestem and tall grass.

As far as I could see, I was entirely alone.

I dismounted and let the horse blow for a moment while I scouted around and listened to the darkness. There was no sign that I could see and nothing that I could hear, but when I remounted and splashed the sorrel through the creek and up onto the far bank, the ground was so churned-up that I'd've had to be blind to miss it.

I swung down, bent and examined the confusion of ruts and tracks. Their edges were still crumbly and the earth itself was still damp, which meant they'd been made recently.

Eagerly now, I looked away to the north. All I could see were dark groves of timber and clusters of rock. But I knew that Jay had taken his sooners that way. There wasn't one shred of doubt about that.

I settled myself back into my saddle and set off at

a steady, wary lope. I felt so close now that I had to fight the urge to hurry. I couldn't rush into this. I had to have a plan of action. I knew that Jay would never give himself up without a fight, so there was the safety of the sooners to consider as well. It was true that they were breaking the law in trying to jump the gun, but they were innocent bystanders as far as the business between Jay and me was concerned, and I had no wish to endanger them.

But the chances were good that Jay would be out ahead of the column, so if I could just overtake him and then come at him from the side …

I started to hear muted sounds from up ahead now, the low rattle and creak of swaying wagons, the odd cry of a restless or frightened child, the occasional bawl of an ox, the clatter and ring of straining harness. I reined down suddenly, for the last wagon was now in sight, no more than a hundred-twenty yards in front of me.

My throat went dry.

Hurriedly I surveyed as much of the land as I could see in the darkness. I had to swing a wide loop around the column and take a better look at it before I made my move, because Jay wouldn't be in this on his own, he'd have someone helping him, maybe a couple of someones.

I let the column push away from me, then clucked the sorrel to a run. We rode west, northwest, north. I reined down again and blew a soft whistle. The slow-moving wagon train was strung out over maybe three-quarters of a mile. That made it a lot of wagons, a hell of a lot.

Ned Brooding's going to be pleased with this little haul, I thought.

I pressed on north, keeping to cover all the

while, until the wagon train lay behind me. Then I turned northwest and finally east, onto a course that would put me directly in front of it.

The land alongside the twisting, oxbow route of Rattler Creek was rocky and uneven now, and long, dry grass shushed and whispered in a tepid night wind as I reined down and searched for a good vantage point. When I found it I angled the horse up across a slope of loose red soil upon which patches of stunted scrub sat like polka dots. At the top I swung down and tethered my horse to some brush, out of sight behind a seamed grey outcrop.

I slid Ned's shotgun from its scabbard, broke it open, found it loaded and snapped it shut again. Next I took a couple of his spare Nitro-Express cartridges from my saddlebags and stuffed them into my pants'-pocket.

At last I was ready.

I traced my tracks back down the slope and stopped about halfway. Here a combination of stubby, spiky brush and oval, pitted boulders meandered across the incline in a drunken line. The spot was perfect for my purpose, because it offered good cover and afforded me a clear view of the rough, flattened-grass trail that ran along beside the burbling creek, no more than eighty feet below.

I hunkered down behind a barrel-sized rock and prepared myself for what I hoped would only be a short wait. I was breathing hard and my stomach was tingling with anticipation. I took out my watch, checked the time and cursed. It was fifteen minutes to midnight. Somehow this whole business had taken longer than it should have, and Ned would have called out the army by now.

I put the watch away and listened to the night. Sweat trickled down one side of my face and made the skin itch.

Suddenly I heard a horse's hoof striking rock, and I turned my attention south, to the trail along which Jay would be leading his sooners.

I caught my breath.

A single rider had walked his horse into sight about forty yards away. He was slouched in his saddle, looking back over his shoulder every couple of seconds.

Jay?

No. No, it was the wrong body-shape for Jay.

Something inside me seemed to sag, and I started to wonder if maybe I'd got it wrong. Maybe Jay was only a front man, the fellow who drummed up all the business but didn't take any of the risks. Maybe he'd never intended to lead these sooners out here himself.

The rider walked his dark horse nearer, and about a dozen yards behind him came the first of the wagons, its high canvas top shuddering and shaking to every dip and bump in the trail.

I turned my attention back to the lead rider. He was close enough for me to see more clearly now. And yet it was his horse that I recognised first, a big black animal with a white blaze on its forehead.

Ed Vallance's horse.

Again the rider turned back to make sure the wagons were still creaking and clanking on, and when he put his gaze back to the front I saw his face and that confirmed it. It was Ed Vallance down there, all right. Sharp Edgar Vallance.

I let my breath go in a soft rush, though I can't honestly say I was surprised. This just made his connection with Jay a little easier to understand, that and the reason he'd been so eager to get me out of the way. If I'd found Jay before Jay had the chance to go out and find a large-enough bunch of sooners, I'd have ruined his whole dirty scheme.

Two other riders suddenly cantered up from further down the line, and I thrust my musing aside. Ed heard them coming and slowed his own horse and turned it sideways on. The two riders pulled in beside him, one of them sitting with his back to me. The other one, a biggish fellow — possibly Cal, one of the pugs I'd fought the night before — said something I didn't catch and pointed back.

I strained hard to hear what they were saying. From what I could gather, one of the sooner wagons had shattered a wheel on some loose rock. That made Ed swear. Then he told them to go back and keep the other wagons moving around it. If the sooner in the busted wagon could get it fixed, he could follow on. If not, that was *his* lousy luck.

Cal — I was certain it was him — bobbed his head and said, 'Come on,' to his companion. And as the pair of them made to turn their animals around, I saw the second man's face for the first time.

Excitement flared up inside me, because it was *him*. Jay.

My daughter's killer.

EIGHT

I knew I was never going to get a better chance
than this, so I threw caution to the wind and came
up with the shotgun in my fists and bawled, *'Hold it,
the lot of you!'*

There was a moment then when everything
stopped. There was no sound ... no movement ...
even the breeze died down and the creek dropped
its chattering to a whisper. As one, three heads
whipped around to look at me, Ed, Cal, Jay. Their
faces were pale ovals, their wide, startled eyes and
shock-loosened mouths just blobs of dark shadow.

I called, *'Put your hands up! You're under arrest!'*

And for a moment there I really thought I was
going to pull it off.

But then —

Cal broke the spell. His face screwed up with a
yell and he went for the gun in his waistband, and
that was too bad because I'd been hoping to keep
the fighting to a minimum so that I could bring Jay
in alive and keep Ned happy.

As Cal snatched for his .45, all three of them split
apart to become moving targets. But because Cal
was the most dangerous man there in that moment
— as well as the most expendable — I concentrated
on him, swinging the Express around and letting

him have the long left-side barrel as a dissuader.

The night was ripped apart by the gun-blast, and I swear the muzzle-flash spat eighteen inches out into the darkness.

BOOOM!

Cal and his prancing horse took the blast in equal measure, and that was a shame because no man worth his salt wants an innocent beast to suffer, but that's the price you pay when you use a shotgun. The damn' things are what they call *indiscriminate*.

Cal and the animal screeched and fell sideways in an explosion of lacerated flesh that made the ground tremble. I yelled too, because the Express packed a hell of a recoil, and it kicked right back up to my already-sore shoulders.

A bullet spanged off the rock in front of me. Instinctively I put my head down as stone chips rained against my hat-brim. I retaliated almost at once, letting go the right-side barrel without aiming, just to give them something to worry about while I ducked back out of sight, broke the weapon open, popped out the two still-smoking empties and stuffed in fresh loads.

More gunfire riddled the night, blending with the panic-sounds now coming from the stalled sooners. In the very next moment there was a lull in the firing and I snapped the Express shut, snaked twelve feet further along the line of cover and came up blasting.

BOOOM! ... BOOOM!

The first thing I saw when the smoke cleared was Ed, trying to control his spooked and rearing mount. The second thing I saw was Jay, jamming his heels into his horse's flanks and getting the hell away from there.

Furious now, I came up over the brush, heedless of safety, and yelled at him to stop, or else. But evidently he figured *or else* was preferable to stopping, because the bastard just kept going.

I broke the Express. Hot empties flipped out and hit the ground with a coppery tinkle. I fumbled in my pocket for reloads, but the heady mixture of fear and excitement made my fingers awkward. At last the reloads pressed cold and curved into my palm, and almost before I knew it I was slotting them home, not liking it but figuring to shoot Jay's horse out from under him before he could get away from me again.

I brought the shotgun up, sighted on the fleeing animal –

Then something punched me in the right arm and I cried out, staggered and dropped the shotgun with a clatter in front of me. Even through the pain I knew right away what had happened. I'd know that watery slap anywhere. I'd been shot again. Dammit, I'd been *shot* again!

The world was tilting on a stormy sea. I glanced down, saw blood staining my shirtsleeve with a ragged red rose. Another shot buzzed close by and my head snapped up. At the foot of the slope, Ed Vallance was trying to turn his sidestepping black horse towards me, his Smith & Wesson .44 smoking in his hand.

I looked at him and saw amazement on his face. Never in his wildest dreams had he ever believed he would hit me, and yet somehow he had – and now he wanted to finish me for good.

Caught up in the excitement of the moment, he loosed off a yell, kicked his horse up to a reckless gallop and came thundering through the tall grass and came up over the loose red earth towards me. His hat flew off in the slipstream, but he ignored it. His eyes were alight with the urge to kill.

The pain in my arm was a crippling thing, but I was truly damned if I'd let him take me without a fight. Doggedly I reached down for the shotgun and somehow straightened back up. Seeing me do that, he kicked his mount to an even greater clip. Its mane whipped this way and that: its eyes showed wide and scared; its foamy lips peeled back to reveal its big, yellow teeth –

I brought the shotgun up, groaning with pain because all of a sudden the weapon weighed a ton. In front of me, dirt and brush exploded up from beneath the horse's pounding hooves. At last, when Ed was no more than forty feet away, I let go one barrel without aiming – BOOOM! – and the horse reared up, spilled Ed out of his saddle ... then kept coming on.

I saw it coming but I just couldn't get out of its way quick enough. It caught me a glancing blow and tossed me to one side. I fell, let go of the shotgun, tasted dirt in my mouth and rolled, trapping another groan behind my teeth as pain scratched ever deeper into my wounded arm.

I came up. The world was still stumbling drunk. From the edge of my vision I saw Ed getting up as well. Ed, winded by the fall, gasping for air, still holding his .44 in his hand.

We looked at each other then, and once again that stretch of Rattler Creek grew silent as something moved in Ed's beady, bright-as-a-button eyes ... recognition. It came to me suddenly that so far, all I'd been to him was a shadow on a hill, an enemy. Only now was he recognising me for the first time, and he just couldn't believe it. He muttered, 'Allison ...?'

Then he raised his gun and tried to shoot me again.

As he did it, I dived for the shotgun, hit the ground, snatched it up, turned it onto him –

The two weapons exploded at the same time. I guess I'll never know where Ed's shot went. As for mine ...

Ed jerked and lumbered backwards down the incline as buckshot peppered his shirtfront and shredded his chest into so many red ribbons. He dropped his gun, keeled over and slid partway down the incline, his limbs loose and uncoopera-tive. At length he came to rest on his back, arms outstretched, bootheels pushing tracks into the dirt as his legs writhed around like two giant worms.

All at once it was over. No more shooting, no more killing, no more screaming. Reaction mixed with pain and loss of blood to make me want to puke, but I held it down. I glanced over at Cal and his horse. Both sprawled and still. I looked for Jay and swore. He was gone, damn him.

Suddenly Ed made a gravelly kind of noise in his throat, and I stumbled down the slope and knelt beside him. His face was chalky, with a line of blood showing at his nose and more glistening on his fleshy lips.

He said, '... All ... isonnn ...'

'I'm here, Ed.'

He looked for me, but his own very personal darkness meant that he couldn't see me, and he frowned. 'S ... sure ... never ... count ... ed ... on ... findin' ... you ... out here ...' he whispered.

I looked down at him and wanted to feel

something for him but couldn't. All I could think about were the seven Chickasaws he'd killed with his lousy rotgut whiskey, and the two occasions when he'd tried to have me killed, once back in '83 and again last night. 'Life is full of surprises, Ed,' I replied after a while.

He nodded sluggishly. 'Well ... I guess ... you sure ... got me ... euchred ... this time.' His breath was a painful laboured sawing. '... guess I shoulda ... let you ... have Jay ... right from the start ... huh?'

'Uh-huh.'

'Well ... you can ... f-feel might ... y ... proud of your ... self now ... Jim. It t-took you ... a time ... but you finally ... got me ... didn't you?'

Again I said, 'Uh-huh.'

A shudder ran through him then, and afterwards he lay dead.

I reached down and closed his eyes, wondering how his death would affect the murder charge I had hanging over me. My guess was that it would be dropped now. Ghoulishly I told myself that Ed had just settled out of court.

I thrust up and turned my thoughts back to Jay. I felt giddy and knew I'd have to patch my arm up before I went much further, but I didn't know how much time I had before the army got here. Men were calling to one another down the line of wagons, trying to find out what was happening, and scared women and children were crying. I looked at the first of the sooners. They were standing beside their wagons with their hands up.

'Stay right where you are!' I called over to them. 'The army's on its way to take you back to Oklahoma Station!'

That started them chattering again.

I turned away from them and went back up the slope, past Ed's black, to catch up my own mount. I slid the shotgun away. My arm hurt like a bitch, but I could flex my fingers okay, so I guessed that meant the damage was minimal.

Another wave of imbalance swept over me as I tried to mount up, and I had to wait a couple of moments for it to pass. Finally I climbed onto the sorrel and we moved off.

Beyond the hill country, the land broke up and turned choppy. I reined down and swore again. Jay could have gone to ground anywhere down there, or lit out in practically any direction for good. There was no way of telling for sure. But as long as he was out there somewhere, I had to keep after him. I couldn't let him get away from me now.

I rode down onto the trail and scanned the ground for sign of him. My eyes felt scratchy and glazed. It had been a long, eventful twenty four hours, and I was bushed. But there could be no rest for me yet. Neither could I afford to linger here much longer, because of the army.

Jay's tracks weren't hard to find. He'd been in too much of a hurry to disguise or otherwise erase them. They followed the contortions of Rattler Creek as it chuckled and burbled ever north, just like I suspicioned they would.

I pulled the Express from leather, tugged out the spent shells, took two fresh rounds from my saddlebag and reloaded. When I set off again, the shotgun was resting across my lap, ready for action.

I rode cautiously through the after-midnight

darkness, anticipating an ambush and trying to stay alert for it, but nothing happened.

About two miles along the trail, Jay's horse veered right, into the creek. I reined down and shook my head in dismay. I'd been afraid he'd do something like that. Unless I could pick up his trail again, he'd as good as given me the slip permanently.

I tooled my sorrel into the water and crossed to the far bank. There were no horse-tracks there, not that I'd really been expecting any, only those of smaller animals.

Where had he gone, then? Hell, the answer to that was simple. He could've gone *anywhere*. North or south, for one mile or a dozen, or maybe just a hundred yards.

Or maybe he'd decided to linger right here and wait for me ...

I looked around, the breath tight in my throat. But no shot crashed out of the darkness, no more of those Godawful watery slaps to lift me out of the saddle.

No. He was gone. Long gone.

My sigh was a soft, expressive, defeated sound.

My right arm had stiffened up and gone numb. Blood had trickled down to dry in sticky rivulets across the back of my hand. I told myself that I'd better clean it up and inspect the wound, else infection might set in and make it infinitely worse.

Much as I wanted to take a look at it, however, I knew I wouldn't see much in the darkness, and I couldn't risk a fire, not even the quick, tell-tale flare of a match. No. My inspection of the damage would, like everything else, have to wait for daybreak.

I gigged the horse on north, to put some more distance between me and the army, and came to a stand of dogwoods sometime around one o'clock. I dismounted, tethered the horse, took a long drink from my canteen and sank down against a cool rock, still holding the shotgun across my knees.

Much as I hated to admit it, there was nothing more I could do about Jay now until first light – and even then I had my doubts about being able to find him in this isolated vastness. I let myself doze lightly, more to make the night pass quicker than anything else, and slept a shallow, dreamless sleep.

I woke up cold and cramped a few hours later, and watched the grey horizon lighten slowly. Then I went down to the creek, pulled my shirt out of my waistband and peeled it off. I washed the dried blood off my arm and inspected the puffy blue skin around the crusted wound. I'm no expert, but I can recognise a bullet-crease when I see one, and when I saw my own, I felt relieved. It was tender, but I could live with that. At least I now knew that I didn't have a chunk of lead in me that would eventually need cutting out.

I tore my soiled shirt into strips and bound the wound as best I could. Then I splashed cold water onto my face to chase away the cobwebs, went back to my grazing horse and put on my spare shirt. By that time the sun was strengthening and I was eager to pick up Jay's trail again.

Before I could do any such thing, I heard the rolling drum of horse-hooves away to the east and hustled back to the timber's edge to find out who it was.

As I'd already guessed, it was an eight-man cavalry patrol, cantering past about three hundred yards away, on the other side of Rattler Creek. I watched them until they were out of sight, wondering if they were here on a routine sweep of the area, or whether Ned had sent them out specifically to find Jay and me.

Thoughtfully I went back to the sorrel and readied him for travel. I was hungry but couldn't spare the time to eat, even supposing I could risk a fire, so I had to make do with a couple of waxy crackers I'd bought along with some other supplies before I'd left Wetherby.

I stayed close to the creek, knowing that Jay would have had to come out again sometime, and hoping to pick up his tracks when he did. But by the time morning had turned to afternoon, I'd still had no luck. I moved away from the creek and cut the country with a series of wide sweeps. Nothing. I came back on the other side of the creek. Still nothing.

In the middle of the afternoon I saw a cavalry patrol riding across the distant horizon, and hurriedly sought cover. It might have been the same patrol I'd seen earlier. I strained my eyes to count them. Six ... seven ... eight. It probably was, then. And so far, at least, they hadn't taken any prisoners.

I rode back to the dogwood trees and spelled myself and the horse. I felt disappointed, and worn down by events. My right arm was still stiff and sore, but it wasn't paining me too much, and I was grateful for that.

I made a rough, temporary camp and watched the long day fade. I had to face the fact that Jay was likely miles away by now. How I was going to find him again, I just didn't know.

I tried to put myself in his position, to think the way *he* would think. He'd want to lose himself in another crowd, a big city maybe. Well … all right. It wasn't going to be easy, but I'd find him again, just the way I'd found him this time. I *had* to. And when I did …

My thoughts drifted to Ned Brooding. He'd know better than to think I'd broken my word to him, but all the same he'd be wondering what had become of me. I filled and lit my pipe. As always, the tobacco calmed me. There was nothing more I could accomplish here in The District, that was obvious. Best thing I could do in the circumstances was to head back to Oklahoma Station in the morning and turn myself in so that we could clear that murder charge up once and for all.

I nodded to myself, my decision made, and flexed the fingers of my stiff right hand.

Yeah. Tomorrow.

For the second night running I made a cold camp, just in case. It was true that Jay was gone. And if the army should find me now … well, I'd decided to head back to Oklahoma Station tomorrow anyway. But there was no point in advertising my presence any more than I had to.

I slept fitfully and was up with the sun next morning. My arm was throbbing and the crease itself itched like hell. I finished the last of my crackers and washed a can of cold beans down with brackish canteen water. Then I saddled the sorrel and moved out.

On the edge of the trees I drew rein and regarded the unending wilderness in a slow pan.

Yesterday I'd quartered the country from here on north without finding a single track. Today I might as well quarter the country from here down to the south, just in case. After all, I had nothing to lose. It was on my route back to Oklahoma Station anyway.

So it began all over again, those endless, broad sweeps first to the west, then back southwest, then southwest again, and so on until, in the end, I was moving down the country in a string of long zig-zags, my eyes – when they weren't on the lookout for army patrols – always on the ground.

I told myself that there was always the chance that Jay could've doubled back on himself, just to confuse me. I doubted it, but you never knew.

Half an hour later I guessed I'd been right to doubt it.

But ninety minutes after that, I found Jay's tracks.

I could hardly believe my luck at first, and I threw myself down off my horse and knelt so that I could examine them closer and confirm that they really were his.

They were pointing southeast, across a great expanse of rippling buffalo grass. I traced them lightly with my fingertips, and tried to match them in my mind with the tracks I'd started following just after the shootout at Rattler Creek.

To anyone but a Westerner, one hoofprint is much the same as another. But it isn't. There are all kinds of subtle differences – *if* you know what to look for.

I knew.

These were the prints of Jay's horse, all right. And made not more than twenty, thirty minutes earlier.

I straightened up, thumb-scratching the hair under my lip and thinking. Lord alone knew why Jay had stuck around these parts as long as he had.

Maybe he'd been looking for *me* all that time, figuring to settle things between us once and for all, rather than spend the rest of his days with me on his trail.

But now ...

Now it looked as if he'd decided to call it a day and was heading back to Oklahoma Station himself.

I reached up and sleeved sweat off my face. As morning closed on noon, the heat was starting to grip the land and its few inhabitants in a scalding fist and squeeze the juices out of both. But I don't suppose that was the only reason I'd started sweating. Anticipation had something to do with it as well.

I turned my eyes back to the southeast and thought, *Twenty or thirty minutes ...*

God, I could hardly believe it.

A far-away sound interrupted my thoughts just then, some kind of a shout, and I snapped my head to the north.

'Damn!'

A cavalry patrol had come to a prancing halt a little more than a third of a mile away on the other side of the wide prairie, and they'd spotted me. I guessed that the yell had come from the officer in command, that he was calling on me to stand fast because I was under arrest, but if he thought I was going to let myself be taken now of all times, then he didn't know Jim Allison.

I snatched up my reins, flung myself up into the saddle and heeled the sorrel into a gallop away from them, and together we tore out of there like a bullet out of a Gatling gun. Above the *chaka-dum, chaka-dum* of my horse's jolting hooves, I heard another shout and risked a look over my shoulder.

The patrol was giving chase.

I cursed them some more, even though I knew they were only doing their duty, and crouched over the sorrel's driving neck as we continued southeast across the grassy sward.

A gunshot slapped out across the flats in a string of echoes. Instinctively I flinched, even though I knew that any warning shots would be aimed skyward. I looked back again. I was right. The officer was standing up in his stirrups and calling upon me to stop. But I couldn't, not now, so I just kept the horse at a gallop and tried to out-distance them some more.

Rattler Creek shimmered and twinkled ahead of us, and the sorrel broke stride because he couldn't see the bottom and didn't know how deep it was. But I kept him running straight for it. I had to. The shaggy bank blundered toward us and reluctantly the horse leapt into the silvery flow. Water burst up around us, soaking us both. The horse stumbled, nearly threw me, then righted himself and kept going, ploughing through the confluence until we both surged up onto the far bank and continued our dripping flight.

I shook water out of my eyes, heard more shouting, another warning gunblast. My only response was to keep urging the sorrel to ever greater efforts.

We went up and over a gentle rise and down the other side with turfs flying up from under the sorrel's pounding hooves. I left my stomach behind, because the drop was steeper than I'd expected, but still the horse kept racing across the now-broken land.

I chanced another glance over my shoulder. The

rise hid the soldiers from my view. I put my eyes back on the trail ahead, saw more rolling grassland. Then –

A shallow dribble of water meandered across the plain. I remembered it from the night before. We splashed madly into it, water exploding everywhere around us in silvery droplets. Then we were back on solid ground again, the horse still running hard.

Again I checked our backtrail. The cavalry patrol was only now spilling down into the broken country. It looked like they'd been as surprised by the steep drop as me. One horse cannoned into another and they both fell and spilled their riders. The rest slipped and skidded down the incline, their riders only just managing to keep their seats.

A jumble of timber loomed up ahead and stretched north and northwest, hemming us in. I sent the sorrel towards it in a stumbling run. Nearer it came, nearer …

The trees reached out and claimed us, and suddenly the horse's hooves were muted by a loamy carpet of damp leaves and I found myself in a twilight world where the brassy sun could not fully penetrate.

I kept the sorrel dodging trees for about three hundred yards, then yanked the reins hard to the right and abruptly we were racing south. A hundred yards further on, I shortened the reins and the horse came to a grateful stop. I slipped down out of the saddle, tugged him over behind a confusion of interlaced trees and brush and put my free hand over his nose.

After that, all we could do was wait, and catch our breath.

We didn't have to wait long. You could've heard that cavalry patrol coming a mile off. All at once the timber came to life with the rumble of the horses, the yells of the men as they urged their mounts to go faster, the exhortations of their officer to keep going. Disturbed birds fluttered from one lofty perch to another, their cries shrill and piercing. Small animals darted or shuffled for cover. Sensing the relative closeness of its own kind, my horse tugged at the reins, but I held him firm.

I looked through the tortured tangle of tree-limbs and caught the odd flash of blue as the patrol blundered on, heading east. The horse tugged some more, and stamped its hooves restively, but I held him still.

The better part of a minute passed ... and then they were gone.

I closed my eyes and wiped fresh sweat off my face with a shaky palm. Around me, silence pressed back in on the forest. I waited for a while, until I was certain they'd gone, then led the horse out from the cover and mounted up. There was no telling how long the soldiers would run before they realised that I was no longer there for the catching. I could only hope it would be long enough.

I walked the horse to the fringes of the timber and scanned the bumpy grasslands beyond. There they went, the troopers, all eight of them strung out in a ragged blue and brown line, chasing off across the plains. I watched them go, smiling coolly.

Then the officer lifted one arm and they slowed to a halt.

I frowned. That was a bad sign. I'd hoped they

would run a long ways from here before they discovered that I'd shaken them off. But maybe I'd underestimated the officer. Maybe he was sharper than I'd thought.

I watched them regroup. The officer held a brief conference with his sergeant, then checked the time on a watch he pulled from inside his tunic. I was sure they were going to turn round and come back for me. If they did, I wasn't sure my horse could outrun them again. He was a good horse, but far from the best, and he'd done well just to outrun those sleek, grainfed army mounts the first time.

Then something happened to make my frown deepen even more. The officer turned his men away to the southwest and led them off at an orderly, unhurried trot.

I couldn't believe my eyes. Were they really giving up the chase? It sure looked that way. For a few moments I wondered why, then thought to hell with it. It was enough that they were leaving, and making no further attempt to run me to ground.

I reached down, unlimbered my canteen and took a long pull. This really *was* turning out to be my lucky day. A few moments later the patrol vanished over another rock- and timber-littered ridge and I was left alone in the silent District. I let my breath out in a shallow sigh, then turned my attention back to Jay.

I was close now. Real close.

I trotted the sorrel through the timber and out into open country. Now that the sun was reaching its peak, the heat struck like an invisible sledgehammer. We crossed a broad dish of land. I searched for tracks, hoping to pick up Jay's, but found nothing. I went up the far slope, down into the next section of dips and swells, scanning the ground through desperate eyes.

After a quarter of an hour I thought, *Dammit, I've lost him again*.

But I couldn't have. Could I? No, not now. Please, Lord, not now …

I sent the sorrel across the vast plain at an easy lope, then let him pick his own path down through the narrow, rocky wash and out into another of those distinctive bowls of rich green grass.

I slowed down, stood up in my stirrups and surveyed my new surroundings. Here and there a redbud or pecan lifted its blossoming branches to heaven. To each distant horizon the pure blue sky met a gentle swell of grass and the odd darker, gnarlier tree. I tried to get my bearings, but the chase had disorientated me a bit and I was no longer entirely sure where I was. Not far from Oklahoma Station, that was certain, but exactly where … I couldn't say.

I heeled the sorrel towards the far southeastern ridge, and as he ran, his shadow tried to stay right beneath him and out of the furnace heat.

I didn't blame it.

We closed on the brushy, rock-studded ridge, and when we were no more than thirty yards from the base of the slope, a rifle shot cracked through the noonday air and the sorrel whinnied, shuddered and began to collapse front-end first.

A lot of things happen in moments like that. Chief among them is confusion. Your mind screams *Who? Why? Where?*, just like mine did. But there's no time for answers right then. They have to wait for later. In that one single instant it's only actions that count.

I kicked out of the stirrups and threw myself sideways as the sorrel hit the dirt on its folded forelegs, and then toppled sideways, bleeding sluggishly from a small, puckered hole in its neck. We both hit the dirt at about the same time, with me landing heavier than I meant to, and as white-hot pain lanced up my left leg from ankle to kneecap, I groaned and lost my balance.

The fall knocked the wind out of me, and there was no time to regain it. I just had to reach the dead horse as fast as I could, because he was all the cover I had. As I bellied through the grass like an oversized snake, I felt something tear in my right arm, the bullet-crease reopening, and I cursed as fresh blood started to stain my sleeve.

The horse was still twelve feet away when the bushwhacker pumped another bullet into the breech and called down, 'Move another inch an' I'll shoot you right here an' now, Allsion!'

I froze there on my hands and knees, sucking in warm air. I'd known who the bushwhacker was right from the start, of course. Hearing his voice now only confirmed his identity. Slowly I raised my head and looked at him.

Yeah, it was him, all right.

Jay Bannon.

He was skylined at the top of the slope, with the sun winking and flaring down at me over one shoulder. In his fists he carried a Henry repeater, which he kept pointed my way. On his face he wore a hard, sadistic smile.

His face. Those dark, look-right-into-you eyes. The long nose. Wide mouth. Weak jaw shaded by stubble. I shook my head at him, too consumed by hatred to fear him.

Without warning I was suddenly transported back through time, to that warm mid-summer's evening when he'd first come into our lives. Then the scene changed. Tom Jessup was saying, 'I don't mind tellin' you, Jim, I'll feel a sight happier when he's gone.'

I heard a noise. *POCK-AH* … *pock-ah* … Jay was hammering the fence-post sideways, his face contorted by illogical rage as he yelled, 'Come on, you bastard!'

Everything else fell into place quickly then, so quickly that it left me feeling a little sick. Wetherby. Connie Crane. My daughter's grave. My grandson, the son Jay himself had so casually abandoned …

I pushed myself up onto my feet, and he took a step back up the incline and levelled the Henry at my belly and said, 'Whoa there, Allison, that's enough of that!'

I made no further moves, and that pleased him.

He gestured with the barrel of the weapon and said, 'Shuck that sidearm.'

I still didn't move.

'Shuck it, I said!'

His voice had a shrill, unbalanced edge to it.

Using the fingertips of my left hand, I took my Colt out of its holster and tossed it aside. That made him feel even better, you could see. And that was just how I wanted him to feel, that he was the big man here, that he was in charge.

'You kill Ed?' he asked conversationally.

I nodded.

'Too bad. He was a pretty good employer.'

'Better than me, Jay?' I asked mildly.

He ignored that. 'I knew you'd come after me,' he said. 'Jim Allison, the big lawman. I bet it was just like old times, wasn't it? Trackin' a feller down?' Suddenly he frowned. 'How'd you find me, anyhow? Here, I mean, not Wetherby. I know all about the letter that bitch of a daughter sent you.'

I shrugged cautiously, because blood was trickling down the back of my right hand and dripping off the tips of my fingers. 'Does it matter?' I asked.

He shook his head, and the long dark hair beneath his disreputable hat grazed the collar of his cheap shirt. 'I guess not. Couple minutes from now an' I'll never have to concern myself with you again.'

My breathing finally settled down to normal, and I thought, *Well, there it is. I'm a dead man, and this is just borrowed time.*

I looked up at him and remembered the promise I'd made to Ned Brooding, that I'd do my best to fetch this smear of slime in alive, and I shook my head again. All at once, the rage and hatred was too much for me to handle. To hell with the word I'd given to Ned, to hell with courts and trials and justice. I wanted to take Jay Bannon and break him the way he'd broken my Clare, and it didn't matter that I was unarmed, because I still had my bare hands, didn't I?

He looked down at me, frowning as he tried to divine my thoughts. I only stared back at him through unblinking eyes. Where was the point in trying to keep my word to an old friend now? Jay was going to kill me – once he was through gloating over the fact. But there was something he didn't know yet.

I was going to take him with me.

I drew down a deep breath and started limping slowly towards the slope, my fists forming by my sides, violence gathering in my face, and when I saw the look he gave me, that scared-rabbit look of his, I wanted to yell aloud, because that's just what I wanted to do, to scare him, and then *break* him ...

'Hold up there, Allison!' he screeched, bringing the Henry up a few inches. 'One more step an' I'll shoot!'

I kept coming, my boots slowly eating up the ninety feet that separated us. 'You're gonna shoot me anyway, aren't you, Jay?' I said in a quiet, calm, deadly voice. 'Hell, least I can do is go down fighting, isn't it?'

'*Hold still!*' he screamed, and I saw the Henry shake in his hands.

His horse, tethered a dozen yards away, stamped uneasily. I heard a rumble of thunder, and guessed it was the blood rushing in my ears. But still I kept putting one foot in front of the other, belly-muscles tensed, expecting a bullet any moment and not really giving a damn, so long as he went down with me.

I opened my mouth and said, very deliberately, 'Come on, you bastard ...'

That struck a note with him, and his cheek twitched. '*Damn you, Allison!*'

As the thunder grew louder, I said again, 'Come on, you bastard ...'

'I'm warnin' you!' he yelled. 'I'll *kill* you, Allison!'

I slapped my chest with my left hand. 'Well, here's your target, Jay.'

... rumble ... Rumble ... RUMBLE ...

'I swear I will!'

Now teeth showed in a snarl. 'Come on, then, you bastard ...'

RUMBLE ... RUMBLE ...

'*Damn* you!'

'*Come on, then!*'

He slapped the Henry up to his cheek and I saw his finger whiten on the trigger and knew that this was it, the end. But then –

That rumbling ... it finally seemed to penetrate the fog that had come down over Jay's brain, and I saw him frown and twist around suddenly, almost against his will. I tensed myself, figuring to sprint the last twenty yards towards him while his back was turned, but before I could do anything at all –

– he screamed.

And in the very next moment, a wagon came hurtling over the ridge, drawn by a wall-eyed six-horse team of horses ... and smashed him down.

Rooted to the spot now, I could only watch it happen. I saw him kind of hunch up and then disappear first beneath the horses' hooves, then the jouncing wagon itself.

It was the last thing I'd expected to happen, and it went through my mind that it wasn't really happening at all, I was just seeing things because of all the blood I'd lost.

But then the wagon came bouncing wildly down the slope, canvas awning shuddering, weathered sideboards groaning, and I saw the look of horror on the driver's face as he realised what he'd done, and I knew it *was* all for real.

He kept his wagon going, slapping the reins mercilessly against his horses' broad, lathery backs and yelling words that didn't exist in any language on earth just to keep them running, and as the wagon blurred past me, the wind of its passage buffeted me sideways.

Next moment more wagons followed that first, they came flying over the ridge in all shapes and sizes, and quickly I ran up the slope and threw myself behind a good-sized rock.

In those next few minutes, the whole world went crazy. Wagons and horseback riders filled the land from one horizon to the other. The air quivered to all the rattles and creaks and yells and whistles. I pressed my hands to my ears, hardly able to hear myself think. But at last I understood what was happening, and why the cavalry patrol had given up their pursuit of me earlier.

It was now well past noon on April 22nd, and someone somewhere had finally triggered the momentous pistol shot that opened The District up for settlement. At last, the hitherto-unassigned lands were there for the claiming, and this *was* the claiming – the Land Rush itself.

How long it went on for I can't say. All I know is that I crouched behind that rock for a long, long time as wagon after wagon crashed recklessly down the slope to either side of me and then swayed perilously on in search of an unclaimed hundred-sixty acres.

Every place I looked, I saw thick-spoked wheels blurring and spinning. There were wagons of every type and galloping horses of every breed. The ground shook so hard as they careered past that smaller rocks were dislodged and tumbled carelessly down the incline. I gagged on the dust the wagons left behind them, and saw several flip over and kill entire families in less time than it takes to blink.

I was transfixed by the spectacle of it, because it was at once a vision that could inspire and horrify, a sight that spoke volumes for one man's optimism and another man's greed.

More wagons overturned in the frantic race. But still more ploughed on in search of good land.

And then ... at last ... it was over. And something like silence settled back across the defiled land.

As the dust slowly settled, I looked out at what the rushers had left behind them. Wrecked wagons, discarded possessions, sprawled bodies, winded horses standing docilely in their shattered traces, the odd saddle-animal, lingering by its fallen rider or favouring a lame leg.

But there was more, of course. This was only part of the picture. By the end of today, farms and towns and cities would have been established. Communities would have been forged, new friendships made. This once-isolated part of the country would never be the same again.

Even so, this was a panorama I didn't want to look at any longer than I had to.

It was a few minutes before I staggered back out into the open and brushed myself down. The wound in my arm had crusted over again, and I found that I could just about support myself on my left leg. I looked around me, and at last my eyes found Jay.

What had once *been* Jay.

Now he was just something red and wet and misshapen, hardly recognisable as a human being at all.

I stood over him ... *it* ... and swallowed hard to keep the crackers and beans in my belly. You

couldn't get more broken than he was now.
Whatever punishment he'd inflicted upon my little
girl had been returned to him tenfold.

Savagely I thought, *Good*.

At last I looked away from him. It didn't bother
me that he hadn't died at my hands after all. It was
enough for me that he *was* dead. And in a way, I
was relieved that it had turned out the way it had,
because of the promise I'd made to Ned.

Ned …

He was going to want to know everything that
had happened out here, and I would tell him, and
then go home to New Mexico and tell my wife all
about it as well. And after that, we would set about
picking up the pieces of our lives and remember
Clare for the wonderful daughter she had always
been.

I went and retrieved my gun and fetched the rest
of my gear from the sorrel. Good horse that, I
thought, and I regretted his death sincerely. Then
I transferred my things to Jay's mount and headed
for Oklahoma Station.

I was tired. Tired in a way that I never used to
be, back when I packed a badge. All of this business
… I was getting too old for it. And I had a
grandson to prove it.

A grandson.

While ever we had him, we still had a part of
Clare with us as well. That was a comforting
thought, a thought I would hold to.

Suddenly I found myself riding towards
Oklahoma Station with a new sense of purpose,
and for the first time in too long, I smiled a smile of
real warmth and anticipation.

I thought, *I'm coming home, Nan. I'm coming home*.

And the first thing I'm gonna do when I get there is bounce that little feller on my knee.